THE
MAGICIANS OF
CAPRONA

Other titles by Diana Wynne Jones

Chrestomanci Series
Charmed Life
Witch Week
The Lives of Christopher Chant
Mixed Magics

Black Maria
A Tale of Time City
Howl's Moving Castle
Castle in the Air
The Homeward Bounders
Archer's Goon
Eight Days of Luke
Dogsbody

For older readers
Fire and Hemlock
Hexwood
The Time of the Ghost

For younger readers
Wild Robert

THE MAGICIANS OF CAPRONA

By

Diana Wynne Jones

Illustrated by Tim Stevens

Collins

An imprint of HarperCollinsPublishers

For John

First published by Macmillan Children's Books 1980
First published in paperback by Collins 2000
Collins is an imprint of HarperCollins*Publishers* Ltd
77-85 Fulham Palace Road, Hammersmith,
London, W6 8JB

The HarperCollins website address is:
www.**fire**and**water**.com

5 7 9 8 6

Text copyright © Diana Wynne Jones 1980
Illustrations copyright © Tim Stevens 2000

ISBN 0 00 675516 X

The author and illustrator assert the moral right to be
identified as the author and illustrator of the work.

Printed and bound in Great Britain by
Omnia Books Limited,
Glasgow

Author's Note

The world of Chrestomanci is not the same as this one. It is a world parallel to ours, where magic is as normal as mathematics, and things are generally more old-fashioned. In Chrestomanci's world, Italy is still divided into numbers of small States, each with its Duke and capital city. In our world, Italy became one united country long ago.

Though the two worlds are not connected in any way, this story somehow got through. But it came with some gaps, and I had to get help filling them. Clare Davis, Gaynor Harvey, Elizabeth Carter and Graham Belsten discovered for me what happened in the magicians' single combat. And my husband, J.A. Burrow, with some advice from Basil Cottle, actually found the true words of the *Angel of Caprona*. I would like to thank them all very much indeed.

CHAPTER ONE

✳

Spells are the hardest thing in the world to get right. This was one of the first things the Montana children learnt. Anyone can hang up a charm, but when it comes to making that charm, whether it is written or spoken or sung, everything has to be just right, or the most impossible things happen.

An example of this is young Angelica Petrocchi, who turned her father bright green by singing a wrong note. It was the talk of all Caprona – indeed of all Italy – for weeks.

The best spells still come from Caprona, in spite of the recent troubles, from the Casa Montana or the Casa Petrocchi. If you are using words that really work, to improve reception on your radio or to grow tomatoes, then the chances are that someone in your family has been on a holiday to Caprona and brought the spell back. The Old Bridge in Caprona is lined with little stone booths, where long coloured envelopes, scrips and scrolls hang from strings like bunting.

You can get spells there from every spell-house in Italy. Each spell is labelled as to its use and stamped with the sign of the house which made it. If you want to find out who made your spell, look among your family papers. If you find a long cherry-coloured scrip stamped with a black leopard, then it came from the Casa Petrocchi. If you find a leaf-green envelope bearing a winged horse, then the House of Montana made it. The spells of both houses are so good that ignorant people think that even the envelopes can work magic. This, of course, is nonsense. For, as Paolo and Tonino Montana were told over and over again, a spell is the right words delivered in the right way.

The great houses of Petrocchi and Montana go back to the first founding of the State of Caprona, seven hundred years or more ago. And they are bitter rivals. They are not even on speaking terms. If a Petrocchi and a Montana meet in one of Caprona's narrow golden-stone streets, they turn their eyes aside and edge past as if they were both walking past a pig-sty. Their children are sent to different schools and warned never, ever to exchange a word with a child from the other house.

Sometimes, however, parties of young men and women of the Montanas and the Petrocchis happen to meet when they are strolling on the wide street called the

Corso in the evenings. When that happens, other citizens take shelter at once. If they fight with fists and stones, that is bad enough, but if they fight with spells, it can be appalling.

An example of this is when the dashing Rinaldo Montana caused the sky to rain cowpats on the Corso for three days. It created great distress among the tourists.

"A Petrocchi insulted me," Rinaldo explained, with his most flashing smile. "And I happened to have a new spell in my pocket."

The Petrocchis unkindly claimed that Rinaldo had misquoted his spell in the heat of the battle. Everyone knew that all Rinaldo's spells were love-charms.

The grown-ups of both houses never explained to the children just what had made the Montanas and the Petrocchis hate one another so. That was a task traditionally left to the older brothers, sisters and cousins. Paolo and Tonino were told the story repeatedly, by their sisters Rosa, Corinna and Lucia, by their cousins Luigi, Carlo, Domenico and Anna, and again by their second-cousins Piero, Luca, Giovanni, Paula, Teresa, Bella, Angelo and Francesco. They told it themselves to six smaller cousins as they grew up. The Montanas were a large family.

Two hundred years ago, the story went, old Ricardo Petrocchi took it into his head that the Duke of Caprona was ordering more spells from the Montanas than from the Petrocchis, and he wrote old Francesco Montana a very insulting letter about it. Old Francesco was so angry that he promptly invited all the Petrocchis to a feast. He had, he said, a new dish he wanted them to try. Then he rolled Ricardo Petrocchi's letter up into long spills and cast one of his strongest spells over it. And it turned into spaghetti. The Petrocchis ate it greedily and were all taken ill, particularly old Ricardo – for nothing disagrees with a person so much as having to eat his own words. He never forgave Francesco Montana, and the two families had been enemies ever since.

"And that," said Lucia, who told the story oftenest, being only a year older than Paolo, "was the origin of spaghetti."

It was Lucia who whispered to them all the terrible heathen customs the Petrocchis had: how they never went to Mass or confessed; how they never had baths or changed their clothes; how none of them ever got married but just – in an even lower whisper – had babies like kittens; how they were apt to drown their unwanted babies, again like kittens, and had even been known to eat unwanted uncles and aunts; and how they were so dirty that you could smell the Casa Petrocchi and hear the flies buzzing right down the Via Sant' Angelo.

There were many other things besides, some of them far worse than these, for Lucia had a vivid imagination. Paolo and Tonino believed every one, and they hated the Petrocchis heartily, though it was years before either of them set eyes on a Petrocchi. When they were both quite small, they did sneak off one morning, down the Via Sant' Angelo almost as far as the New Bridge, to look at the Casa Petrocchi. But there was no smell and no flies buzzing to guide them, and their sister Rosa found them before they found it. Rosa, who was eight years older than Paolo and quite grown-up even then, laughed when they explained their difficulty, and good-naturedly took them to the Casa Petrocchi. It was in the Via Cantello, not the Via Sant' Angelo at all.

Paolo and Tonino were most disappointed in it. It was just like the Casa Montana. It was large, like the Casa Montana, and built of the same golden stone of Caprona, and probably just as old. The great front gate was old knotty wood, just like their own, and there was even the same golden figure of the Angel on the wall above the gate. Rosa told them that both Angels were in memory of the Angel who had come to the first Duke of Caprona bringing a scroll of music from Heaven – but the boys knew that. When Paolo pointed out that the Casa Petrocchi did not seem to smell much, Rosa bit her lip and said gravely that there were not many windows in the outside walls, and they were all shut.

"I expect everything happens round the yard inside, just like it does in our Casa," she said. "Probably all the smelling goes on in there."

They agreed that it probably did, and wanted to wait to see a Petrocchi come out. But Rosa said she thought that would be most unwise, and pulled them away. The boys looked over their shoulders as she dragged them off and saw that the Casa Petrocchi had four golden-stone towers, one at each corner, where the Casa Montana only had one, over the gate.

"It's because the Petrocchis are show-offs," Rosa said, dragging. "Come on."

Since the towers were each roofed with a little hat of red pantiles, just like their own roofs or the roofs of all the houses in Caprona, Paolo and Tonino did not think they were particularly grand, but they did not like to argue with Rosa. Feeling very let down, they let her drag them back to the Casa Montana and pull them through their own large knotty gate into the bustling yard beyond. There Rosa left them and ran up the steps to the gallery, shouting, "Lucia! Lucia, where are you? I want to *talk* to you!"

Doors and windows opened into the yard all round, and the gallery, with its wooden railings and pantiled roof, ran round three sides of the yard and led to the rooms on the top floor. Uncles, aunts, cousins large and small, and cats were busy everywhere, laughing, cooking, discussing spells, washing, sunning themselves or playing. Paolo gave a sigh of contentment and picked up the nearest cat.

"I don't think the Casa Petrocchi *can* be anything like this inside."

Before Tonino could agree, they were swooped on lovingly by Aunt Maria, who was fatter than Aunt Gina, but not as fat as Aunt Anna. "Where have you been, my loves? I've been ready for your lessons for half an hour or more!"

Everyone in the Casa Montana worked very hard. Paolo and Tonino were already being taught the first rules for making spells. When Aunt Maria was busy, they were taught by their father, Antonio. Antonio was the eldest son of Old Niccolo, and would be head of the Casa Montana when Old Niccolo died. Paolo thought this weighed on his father. Antonio was a thin, worried person who laughed less often than the other Montanas. He was different. One of the differences was that, instead of letting Old Niccolo carefully choose a wife for him from a spell-house in Italy, Antonio had gone on a visit to England and come back married to Elizabeth. Elizabeth taught the boys music.

"If I'd been teaching that Angelica Petrocchi," she was fond of saying, "she'd never have turned anything green."

Old Niccolo said Elizabeth was the best musician in Caprona. And that, Lucia told the boys, was why Antonio got away with marrying her. But Rosa told them to take no notice. Rosa was proud of being half English.

Paolo and Tonino were probably prouder to be Montanas. It was a grand thing to know you were born into a family that was known world-wide as the greatest spell-house in Europe – if you did not count the Petrocchis. There were times when Paolo could hardly wait to grow up and be like his cousin, dashing Rinaldo. Everything came easily to Rinaldo. Girls fell in love with him, spells dripped from his pen. He had composed seven new charms before he left school. And these days, as Old Niccolo said, making a new spell was not easy. There were so many already. Paolo admired Rinaldo desperately. He told Tonino that Rinaldo was a true Montana.

Tonino agreed, because he was more than a year younger than Paolo and valued Paolo's opinions, but it always seemed to him that it was Paolo who was the true Montana. Paolo was as quick as Rinaldo. He could learn without trying spells which took Tonino days to acquire.

Tonino was slow. He could only remember things if he went over them again and again. It seemed to him that Paolo had been born with an instinct for magic which he just did not have himself.

Tonino was sometimes quite depressed about his slowness. Nobody else minded in the least. All his sisters, even the studious Corinna, spent hours helping him. Elizabeth assured him he never sang out of tune. His father scolded him for working too hard, and Paolo assured him that he would be streets ahead of the other children when he went to school. Paolo had just started school. He was as quick at ordinary lessons as he was at spells.

But when Tonino started school, he was just as slow there as he was at home. School bewildered him. He did not understand what the teachers wanted him to do. By the first Saturday he was so miserable that he had to slip away from the Casa and wander round Caprona in tears. He was missing for hours.

"I can't help being quicker than he is!" Paolo said, almost in tears too.

Aunt Maria rushed at Paolo and hugged him. "Now, now, don't you start too! You're as clever as my Rinaldo, and we're all proud of you."

"Lucia, go and look for Tonino," said Elizabeth. "Paolo, you mustn't worry so. Tonino's soaking up spells without knowing he is. I did the same when I came here. Should I tell Tonino?" she asked Antonio. Antonio had hurried in from the gallery. In the Casa Montana, if anyone was in distress, it always fetched the rest of the family.

Antonio rubbed his forehead. "Perhaps. Let's go and ask Old Niccolo. Come on, Paolo."

Paolo followed his thin, brisk father through the patterns of sunlight in the gallery and into the blue coolness of the Scriptorium. Here his other two sisters, Rinaldo and five other cousins, and two of his uncles, were all standing at tall desks copying spells out of big leather-bound books. Each book had a brass lock on it so that the family secrets could not be stolen. Antonio and Paolo tiptoed through. Rinaldo smiled at them without pausing in his copying. Where other pens scratched and paused, Rinaldo's raced.

In the room beyond the Scriptorium, Uncle Lorenzo and Cousin Domenico were stamping winged horses on leaf-green envelopes. Uncle Lorenzo looked keenly at their faces as they passed and decided that the trouble was not too much for Old Niccolo alone. He winked at Paolo and threatened to stamp a winged horse on him.

Old Niccolo was in the warm mildewy library beyond, consulting over a book on a stand with Aunt Francesca. She was Old Niccolo's sister, and therefore really a great-aunt. She was a barrel of a lady, twice as fat as Aunt Anna and even more passionate than Aunt Gina. She was saying passionately, "But the spells of the Casa Montana always have a certain elegance. This is graceless! This is—"

Both round old faces turned towards Antonio and Paolo. Old Niccolo's face, and his eyes in it, were round and wondering as the latest baby's. Aunt Francesca's face was too small for her huge body, and her eyes were small and shrewd. "I was just coming," said Old Niccolo. "I thought it was Tonino in trouble, but you bring me Paolo."

"Paolo's not in trouble," said Aunt Francesca.

Old Niccolo's round eyes blinked at Paolo. "Paolo," he said, "what your brother feels is not your fault."

"No," said Paolo. "I think it's school really."

"We thought that perhaps Elizabeth could explain to Tonino that he can't avoid learning spells in this Casa," Antonio suggested.

"But Tonino has ambition!" cried Aunt Francesca.

"I don't think he does," said Paolo.

"No, but he is unhappy," said his grandfather. "And we must think how best to comfort him. I know." His baby face beamed. "Benvenuto."

Though Old Niccolo did not say this loudly, someone in the gallery immediately shouted, "Old Niccolo wants Benvenuto!" There was running and calling down in the yard. Somebody beat on a water butt with a stick. "Benvenuto! Where's that cat got to? Benvenuto!"

Naturally, Benvenuto took his time coming. He was boss cat at the Casa Montana. It was five minutes before Paolo heard his firm pads trotting along the tiles of the gallery roof. This was followed by a heavy thump as Benvenuto made the difficult leap down, across the gallery railing on to the floor of the gallery. Shortly, he appeared on the library windowsill.

"So there you are," said Old Niccolo. "I was just going to get impatient."

Benvenuto at once shot forward a shaggy black hind

leg and settled down to wash it, as if that was what he had come there to do.

"Ah no, please," said Old Niccolo. "I need your help."

Benvenuto's wide yellow eyes turned to Old Niccolo. He was not a handsome cat. His head was unusually wide and blunt, with grey gnarled patches on it left over from many, many fights. Those fights had pulled his ears down over his eyes, so that Benvenuto always looked as if he were wearing a ragged brown cap. A hundred bites had left those ears notched like holly leaves. Just over his nose, giving his face a leering, lop-sided look, were three white patches. Those had nothing to do with Benvenuto's position as boss cat in a spell-house. They were the result of his partiality for steak. He had got under Aunt Gina's feet when she was cooking, and Aunt Gina had spilt hot fat on his head. For this reason, Benvenuto and Aunt Gina always pointedly ignored one another.

"Tonino is unhappy," said Old Niccolo.

Benvenuto seemed to feel this worthy of his attention. He withdrew his projecting leg, dropped to the library floor and arrived on top of the bookstand, all in one movement, without seeming to flex a muscle. There he stood, politely waving the one beautiful thing about him – his bushy black tail. The rest of his coat had worn to a ragged brown. Apart from the tail, the only thing which showed Benvenuto had once been a magnificent black Persian was the fluffy fur on his hind legs. And, as every other cat in Caprona knew to its cost, those fluffy breeches concealed muscles like a bulldog's.

Paolo stared at his grandfather talking face to face with

Benvenuto. He had always treated Benvenuto with respect himself, of course. It was well known that Benvenuto would not sit on your knee, and scratched you if you tried to pick him up. He knew all cats helped spells on wonderfully. But he had not realised before that cats understood so much. And he was sure Benvenuto was answering Old Niccolo, from the listening sort of pauses his grandfather made. Paolo looked at his father to see if this was true. Antonio was very ill at ease. And Paolo understood from his father's worried face, that it was very important to be able to understand what cats said, and that Antonio never could. I shall have to start learning to understand Benvenuto, Paolo thought, very troubled.

"Which of you would you suggest?" asked Old Niccolo. Benvenuto raised his right front paw and gave it a casual lick. Old Niccolo's face curved into his beaming baby's smile. "Look at that!" he said. "He'll do it himself!"

Benvenuto flicked the tip of his tail sideways. Then he was gone, leaping back to the window so fluidly and quickly that he might have been a paintbrush painting a dark line in the air. He left Aunt Francesca and Old Niccolo beaming, and Antonio still looking unhappy. "Tonino is taken care of," Old Niccolo announced. "We shall not worry again unless he worries us."

CHAPTER TWO

＊

*T*onino was already feeling soothed by the bustle in the golden streets of Caprona. In the narrower streets, he walked down the crack of sunlight in the middle, with washing flapping overhead, playing that it was sudden death to tread on the shadows. In fact, he died a number of times before he got as far as the Corso. A crowd of tourists pushed him off the sun once. So did two carts and a carriage. And once, a long, gleaming car came slowly growling along, hooting hard to clear the way.

When he was near the Corso, Tonino heard a tourist say in English, "Oh look! Punch and Judy!" Very smug at being able to understand, Tonino dived and pushed and tunnelled until he was at the front of the crowd and able to watch Punch beat Judy to death at the top of his little painted sentry-box. He clapped and cheered, and when someone puffed and panted into the crowd too, and pushed him aside, Tonino was as indignant as the rest. He had quite forgotten he was miserable. "Don't shove!" he shouted.

"Have a heart!" protested the man. "I must see Mr Punch cheat the Hangman."

"Then be quiet!" roared everyone, Tonino included.

"I only said—" began the man. He was a large damp-faced person, with an odd excitable manner.

"Shut up!" shouted everyone.

The man panted and grinned and watched with his mouth open Punch attack the policeman. He might have been the smallest boy there. Tonino looked irritably sideways at him and decided the man was probably an amiable lunatic. He let out such bellows of laughter at the smallest jokes, and he was so oddly dressed. He was wearing a shiny red silk suit with flashing gold buttons and glittering medals. Instead of the usual tie, he had white cloth folded at his neck, held in place by a brooch which winked like a tear-drop. There were glistening buckles on his shoes, and golden rosettes at his knees. What with his sweaty face and his white shiny teeth showing as he laughed, the man glistened all over.

Mr Punch noticed him too. "Oh what a clever fellow!" he crowed, bouncing about on his little wooden shelf. "I see gold buttons. Can it be the Pope?"

"Oh no it isn't!" bellowed Mr Glister, highly delighted.

"Can it be the Duke?" cawed Mr Punch.

"Oh no it isn't!" roared Mr Glister, and everyone else.

"Oh yes it is," crowed Mr Punch.

While everyone was howling "*Oh no it isn't!*" two worried-looking men pushed their way through the people to Mr Glister.

"Your Grace," said one, "the Bishop reached the Cathedral half an hour ago."

"Oh bother!" said Mr Glister. "Why are you lot always bullying me? Can't I just – until this ends? I love Punch and Judy."

The two men looked at him reproachfully.

"Oh – very well," said Mr Glister. "You two pay the showman. Give everyone here something." He turned and went bounding away into the Corso, puffing and panting.

For a moment, Tonino wondered if Mr Glister was actually the Duke of Caprona. But the two men made no attempt to pay the showman, or anyone else. They simply went trotting demurely after Mr Glister, as if they were afraid of losing him. From this, Tonino gathered that Mr Glister was indeed a lunatic – a rich one – and they were humouring him.

"Mean things!" crowed Mr Punch, and set about tricking the Hangman into being hanged instead of him. Tonino watched until Mr Punch bowed and retired in triumph into the little painted villa at the back of his stage. Then he turned away, remembering his unhappiness.

He did not feel like going back to the Casa Montana. He did not feel like doing anything particularly. He wandered on, the way he had been going, until he found himself in the Piazza Nuova, up on the hill at the western end of the city. Here he sat gloomily on the parapet, gazing across the River Voltava at the rich villas and the Ducal Palace, and at the long arches of the New Bridge, and wondering if he was going to spend the rest of his life in a fog of stupidity.

The Piazza Nuova had been made at the same time as the New Bridge, about seventy years ago, to give everyone the grand view of Caprona Tonino was looking at now. It was breathtaking. But the trouble was, everything Tonino looked at had something to do with the Casa Montana.

Take the Ducal Palace, whose golden-stone towers cut clear lines into the clean blue of the sky opposite. Each golden tower swept outwards at the top, so that the soldiers on the battlements, beneath the snapping red and gold flags, could not be reached by anyone climbing up from below. Tonino could see the shields built into the battlements, two a side, one cherry, one leaf-green, showing that the Montanas and the Petrocchis had added a spell to defend each tower. And the great white marble front below was inlaid with other marbles, all colours of the rainbow. And among those colours were cherry-red and leaf-green.

The long golden villas on the hillside below the Palace each had a leaf-green or cherry-red disc on their walls. Some were half hidden by the dark spires of the elegant little trees planted in front of them, but Tonino knew they were there. And the stone and metal arches of the New Bridge, sweeping away from him towards the villas and the Palace, each bore an enamel plaque, green and red alternately. The New Bridge had been sustained by the strongest spells the Casa Montana and the Casa Petrocchi could produce.

At the moment, when the river was just a shingly trickle, they did not seem necessary. But in winter, when the rain fell in the Apennines, the Voltava became a furious torrent. The arches of the New Bridge barely cleared it. The Old Bridge – which Tonino could see by craning out and sideways – was often under water, and the funny little houses along it could not be used. Only Montana and Petrocchi spells deep in its foundations stopped the Old Bridge being swept away.

Tonino had heard Old Niccolo say that the New Bridge spells had taken the entire efforts of the entire Montana family. Old Niccolo had helped make them when he was the same age as Tonino. Tonino could not have done. Miserable, he looked down at the golden walls and red pantiles of Caprona below. He was quite certain that every single one hid at least a leaf-green scrip. And the most Tonino had ever done was help stamp the winged horse on the outside. He was fairly sure that was all he ever would do.

He had a feeling somebody was calling him. Tonino looked round at the Piazza Nuova. Nobody. Despite the view, the Piazza was too far for the tourists to come. All Tonino could see were the mighty iron griffins which reared up at intervals all round the parapet, reaching iron paws to the sky. More griffins tangled into a fighting heap in the centre of the square to make a fountain. And even here, Tonino could not get away from his family. A little metal plate was set into the stone beneath the huge iron claws of the nearest griffin. It was leaf-green. Tonino found he had burst into tears.

Among his tears, he thought for a moment that one of the more distant griffins had left its stone perch and come trotting round the parapet towards him. It had left its wings behind, or else had them tightly folded. He was told, a little smugly, that cats do not need wings. Benvenuto sat down on the parapet beside him, staring accusingly.

Tonino had always been thoroughly in awe of Benvenuto. He stretched out a hand to him timidly. "Hallo, Benvenuto."

Benvenuto ignored the hand. It was covered with water from Tonino's eyes, he said, and it made a cat wonder why Tonino was being so silly.

"There are our spells everywhere," Tonino explained. "And I'll never be able— Do you think it's because I'm half English?"

Benvenuto was not sure quite what difference that made. All it meant, as far as he could see, was that Paolo had blue eyes like a Siamese and Rosa had white fur—

"Fair hair," said Tonino.

—and Tonino himself had tabby hair, like the pale stripes in a tabby, Benvenuto continued, unperturbed. And those were all cats, weren't they?

"But I'm so stupid—" Tonino began.

Benvenuto interrupted that he had heard Tonino chattering with those kittens yesterday, and he had thought Tonino was a good deal cleverer than they were. And before Tonino went and objected that those were only kittens, wasn't Tonino only a kitten himself?

At this, Tonino laughed and dried his hand on his trousers. When he held the hand out to Benvenuto again, Benvenuto rose up, very high on all four paws, and advanced to it, purring. Tonino ventured to stroke him. Benvenuto walked round and round, arched and purring, like the smallest and friendliest kitten in the Casa. Tonino found himself grinning with pride and pleasure. He could tell from the waving of Benvenuto's brush of a tail, in majestic, angry twitches, that Benvenuto did not altogether like being stroked – which made it all the more of an honour.

That was better, Benvenuto said. He minced up to Tonino's bare legs and installed himself across them, like a brown muscular mat. Tonino went on stroking him. Prickles came out of one end of the mat and treadled painfully at Tonino's thighs. Benvenuto continued to purr. Would Tonino look at it this way, he wondered, that they were both, boy and cat, a part of the most famous Casa in Caprona, which in turn was part of the most special of all the Italian States?

"I know that," said Tonino. "It's because I think it's wonderful too that I— Are we really so special?"

Of course, purred Benvenuto. And if Tonino were to lean out and look across at the Cathedral, he would see why.

Obediently, Tonino leaned and looked. The huge marble bubbles of the Cathedral domes leapt up from among the houses at the end of the Corso. He knew there never was such a building as that. It floated, high and white and gold and green. And on the top of the highest dome the sun flashed on the great golden figure of the Angel, poised there with spread wings, holding in one hand a golden scroll. It seemed to bless all Caprona.

That Angel, Benvenuto informed him, was there as a sign that Caprona would be safe as long as everyone sang the tune of the Angel of Caprona. The Angel had brought that song in a scroll straight from Heaven to the First Duke of Caprona, and its power had banished the White Devil and made Caprona great. The White Devil had been prowling round Caprona ever since, trying to get back into the city, but as long as the Angel's song was sung, it would never succeed.

"I know that," said Tonino. "We sing the *Angel* every day at school." That brought back the main part of his misery. "They keep making me learn the story – and all sorts of things – and I can't, because I know them already, so I can't learn properly."

Benvenuto stopped purring. He quivered, because Tonino's fingers had caught in one of the many lumps of matted fur in his coat. Still quivering, he demanded rather sourly why it hadn't occurred to Tonino to *tell* them at school that he knew these things.

"Sorry!" Tonino hurriedly moved his fingers. "But," he explained, "they keep saying you have to do them this way, or you'll never learn properly."

Well, it was up to Tonino of course, Benvenuto said, still irritable, but there seemed no point in learning things twice. A cat wouldn't stand for it. And it was about time they were getting back to the Casa.

Tonino sighed. "I suppose so. They'll be worried."

He gathered Benvenuto into his arms and stood up.

Benvenuto liked that. He purred. And it had nothing to do with the Montanas being worried. The aunts would be cooking lunch, and Tonino would find it easier than Benvenuto to nick a nice piece of veal.

That made Tonino laugh. As he started down the steps to the New Bridge, he said, "You know, Benvenuto, you'd be a lot more comfortable if you let me get those lumps out of your coat and comb you a bit."

Benvenuto stated that anyone trying to comb him would get raked with every claw he possessed.

"A brush then?"

Benvenuto said he would consider that.

It was here that Lucia encountered them. She had looked for Tonino all over Caprona by then and she was prepared to be extremely angry. But the sight of Benvenuto's evil lop-sided countenance staring at her out of Tonino's arms left her with almost nothing to say. "We'll be late for lunch," she said.

"No we won't," said Tonino. "We'll be in time for you to stand guard while I steal Benvenuto some veal."

"Trust Benvenuto to have it all worked out," said Lucia. "What is this? The start of a profitable relationship?"

You could put it that way, Benvenuto told Tonino. "You could put it that way," Tonino said to Lucia.

At all events, Lucia was sufficiently impressed to engage Aunt Gina in conversation while Tonino got Benvenuto his veal. And everyone was too pleased to see Tonino safely back to mind too much. Corinna and Rosa minded, however, that afternoon, when Corinna lost her scissors and Rosa her hairbrush. Both of them stormed out on to the gallery. Paolo was there, watching Tonino gently and carefully snip the mats out of Benvenuto's coat. The hairbrush lay beside Tonino, full of brown fur.

"And you can really understand everything he says?" Paolo was saying.

"I can understand all the cats," said Tonino. "Don't move, Benvenuto. This one's right on your skin."

It says volumes for Benvenuto's status – and therefore for Tonino's – that neither Rosa nor Corinna dared say a word to him. They turned on Paolo instead. "What do you mean, Paolo, standing there letting him mess that brush up? Why couldn't you make him use the kitchen scissors?"

Paolo did not mind. He was too relieved that he was not going to have to learn to understand cats himself. He would not have known how to begin.

From that time forward, Benvenuto regarded himself as Tonino's special cat. It made a difference to both of them. Benvenuto, what with constant brushing – for Rosa bought Tonino a special hairbrush for him – and almost as constant supplies filched from under Aunt Gina's nose, soon began to look younger and sleeker. Tonino forgot he had ever been unhappy. He was now a proud and special person. When Old Niccolo needed Benvenuto, he had to ask Tonino first. Benvenuto flatly refused to do anything for anyone without Tonino's permission. Paolo was very amused at how angry Old Niccolo got.

"That cat has just taken advantage of me!" he

stormed. "I ask him to do me a kindness and what do I get? Ingratitude!"

In the end, Tonino had to tell Benvenuto that he was to consider himself at Old Niccolo's service while Tonino was at school. Otherwise Benvenuto simply disappeared for the day. But he always, unfailingly, reappeared around half-past three, and sat on the water butt nearest the gate, waiting for Tonino. And as soon as Tonino came through the gate, Benvenuto would jump into his arms.

This was true even at the times when Benvenuto was not available to anyone. That was mostly at full moon, when the lady cats wauled enticingly from the roofs of Caprona.

Tonino went to school on Monday, having considered Benvenuto's advice. And, when the time came when they gave him a picture of a cat and said the shapes under it went: Ker-a-ter, Tonino gathered up his courage and whispered, "Yes. It's a C and an A and a T. I know how to read."

His teacher, who was new to Caprona, did not know what to make of him, and called the Headmistress. "Oh," she was told. "It's another Montana. I should have warned you. They all know how to read. Most of them know Latin too – they use it a lot in their spells – and some of them know English as well. You'll find they're about average with sums, though."

So Tonino was given a proper book while the other children learnt their letters. It was too easy for him. He finished it in ten minutes and had to be given another.

And that was how he discovered about books. To Tonino, reading a book soon became an enchantment above any spell. He could never get enough of it. He ransacked the Casa Montana and the Public Library, and he spent all his pocket money on books. It soon became well known that the best present you could give Tonino was a book – and the best book would be about the unimaginable situation where there were no spells. For Tonino preferred fantasy. In his favourite books, people had wild adventures with no magic to help or hinder them.

Benvenuto thoroughly approved. While Tonino read, he kept still, and a cat could be comfortable sitting on him. Paolo teased Tonino a little about being such a bookworm, but he did not really mind. He knew he could always persuade Tonino to leave his book if he really wanted him.

Antonio was worried. He worried about everything. He was afraid Tonino was not getting enough exercise. But everyone else in the Casa said this was nonsense. They were proud of Tonino. He was as studious as Corinna, they said, and, no doubt, both of them would end up at Caprona University, like Great-Uncle Umberto. The Montanas always had someone at the University. It meant they were not selfishly keeping the Theory of Magic to the family, and it was also very useful to have access to the spells in the University Library.

Despite these hopes for him, Tonino continued to be slow at learning spells and not particularly quick at school. Paolo was twice as quick at both. But as the years went by, both of them accepted it. It did not worry them. What worried them far more was their gradual discovery that things were not altogether well in the Casa Montana, nor in Caprona either.

CHAPTER THREE

✸

*I*t was Benvenuto who first worried Tonino. Despite all the care Tonino gave him, he became steadily thinner and more ragged again. Now Benvenuto was roughly the same age as Tonino. Tonino knew that was old for a cat, and at first he assumed that Benvenuto was just feeling his years. Then he noticed that Old Niccolo had taken to looking almost as worried as Antonio, and that Uncle Umberto called on him from the University almost every day. Each time he did, Old Niccolo or Aunt Francesca would ask for Benvenuto and Benvenuto would come back tired out. So he asked Benvenuto what was wrong.

Benvenuto's reply was that they might let a cat have some peace, even if the Duke was a booby. And he was not going to be pestered by Tonino into the bargain.

Tonino consulted Paolo, and found Paolo worried too. Paolo had been noticing his mother. Her fair hair had lately become several shades paler with all the white in it, and she looked nervous all the time. When Paolo asked Elizabeth what was the matter, she said, "Oh nothing, Paolo – only all this makes it *so* difficult to find a husband for Rosa."

Rosa was now eighteen. The entire Casa was busy discussing a husband for her, and there did, now Paolo noticed, seem much more fuss and anxiety about the matter than there had been over Cousin Claudia, three years before. Montanas had to be careful who they married. It stood to reason. They had to marry someone who had some talent at least for spells or music; and it had to be someone the rest of the family liked; and, above all, it had to be someone with no kind of connection with the Petrocchis. But Cousin Claudia had found and married Arturo without all the discussion and worry that was going on over Rosa. Paolo could only suppose the reason was "all this", whatever Elizabeth had meant by that.

Whatever the reason, argument raged. Anxious Antonio talked of going to England and consulting someone called Chrestomanci about it. "We want a really strong spell-maker for her," he said. To which Elizabeth replied that Rosa was Italian and should marry an Italian. The rest of the family agreed, except that they said the Italian must be from Caprona. So the question was who.

Paolo, Lucia and Tonino had no doubt. They wanted Rosa to marry their cousin Rinaldo. It seemed to them entirely fitting. Rosa was lovely, Rinaldo handsome, and none of the usual objections could possibly be made. There were two snags, however. The first was that Rinaldo showed no interest in Rosa. He was at present desperately in love with a real English girl – her name was Jane Smith, and Rinaldo had some difficulty pronouncing it – and she had come to copy some of the pictures in the Art Gallery down on the Corso. She was a romantic girl. To please her, Rinaldo had taken to wearing black, with a red scarf at his neck, like a bandit. He was said to be considering growing a bandit moustache too. All of which left him with no time for a cousin he had known all his life.

The other snag was Rosa herself. She had never cared for Rinaldo. And she seemed to be the only person in the Casa who was entirely unconcerned about who she would marry. When the argument raged loudest, she would shake the blonde hair on her shoulders and smile. "To listen to you all," she said, "anyone would think I have no say in the matter at all. It's really funny."

All that autumn, the worry in the Casa Montana grew. Paolo and Tonino asked Aunt Maria what it was all about. Aunt Maria at first said that they were too young to understand. Then, since she had moments when she was as passionate as Aunt Gina or even Aunt Francesca, she told them suddenly and fervently that Caprona was going to the dogs.

"Everything's going wrong for us," she said. "Money's short, tourists don't come here, and we get weaker every year. Here are Florence, Pisa and Siena all gathering round like vultures, and each year one of them gets a few more square miles of Caprona. If this goes on we shan't be a

State any more. And on top of it all, the harvest failed this year. It's all the fault of those degenerate Petrocchis, I tell you! Their spells don't work any more. We Montanas can't hold Caprona up on our own! And the Petrocchis don't even try! They just keep turning things out in the same old way, and going from bad to worse. You can see they are, or that child wouldn't have been able to turn her father green!"

This was disturbing enough. And it seemed to be plain fact. All the years Paolo and Tonino had been at school, they had grown used to hearing that there had been this concession to Florence; that Pisa had demanded that agreement over fishing rights; or that Siena had raised taxes on imports to Caprona. They had grown too used to it to notice. But now it all seemed ominous. And worse shortly followed. News came that the Old Bridge had been seriously cracked by the winter floods.

This news caused the Casa Montana real dismay. For that bridge should have held. If it gave, it meant that the Montana charms in the foundations had given too. Aunt Francesca ran shrieking into the yard. "Those degenerate Petrocchis! They can't even sustain an old spell now! We've been betrayed!"

Though no one else put it quite that way, Aunt Francesca probably spoke for the whole family.

As if that was not enough, Rinaldo set off that evening to visit his English girl, and was led back to the Casa streaming with blood, supported by his cousins Carlo and Giovanni. Rinaldo, using curse words Paolo and Tonino had never heard before, was understood to say he had met some Petrocchis. He had called them degenerate. And it was Aunt Maria's turn to rush shrieking through the yard, shouting dire things about the Petrocchis. Rinaldo was the apple of Aunt Maria's eye.

Rinaldo had been bandaged and put to bed, when Antonio and Uncle Lorenzo came back from viewing the damage to the Old Bridge. Both looked very serious. Old Guido Petrocchi himself had been there, with the Duke's contractor, Mr Andretti. Some very deep charms had given. It was going to take the whole of both families, working in shifts, at least three weeks to mend them.

"We could have used Rinaldo's help," Antonio said.

Rinaldo swore that he was well enough to get out of bed and help the next day, but Aunt Maria would not hear of it. Nor would the doctor. So the rest of the family was divided into shifts, and work went on day and night. Paolo, Lucia and Corinna went to the bridge straight from school every day. Tonino did not. He was still too slow to be much use. But from what Paolo told him, he did not think he was missing much. Paolo simply could not keep up with the furious pace of the spells. He was put to running errands, like poor Cousin Domenico. Tonino felt very sympathetic towards Domenico. He was the opposite of his dashing brother Rinaldo in every way, and he could not keep up with the pace of things either.

Work had been going on, often in pouring rain, for nearly a week, when the Duke of Caprona summoned Old Niccolo to speak to him.

Old Niccolo stood in the yard and tore what was left of his hair. Tonino laid down his book (it was called

Machines of Death and quite fascinating) and went to see if he could help.

"Ah, Tonino," said Old Niccolo, looking at him with the face of a grieving baby. "I have gigantic problems. Everyone is needed on the Old Bridge, and that ass Rinaldo is lying in bed, and I have to go before the Duke with *some* of my family. The Petrocchis have been summoned too. We cannot appear less than they are, after all. Oh *why* did Rinaldo choose such a time to shout stupid insults?"

Tonino had no idea what to say, so he said, "Shall I get Benvenuto?"

"No, no," said Old Niccolo, more upset than ever. "The Duchess cannot abide cats. Benvenuto is no use here. I shall have to take those who are no use on the bridge. You shall go, Tonino, and Paolo and Domenico, and I shall take your uncle Umberto to look wise and weighty. Perhaps that way we shan't look so very thin."

This was perhaps not the most flattering of invitations, but Tonino and Paolo were delighted nevertheless. They were delighted even though it rained hard the next day, the drilling white rain of winter. The dawn shift came in from the Old Bridge under shiny umbrellas, damp and disgruntled. Instead of resting, they had to turn to and get the party ready for the Palace.

The Montana family coach was dragged from the coach-house to a spot under the gallery, where it was carefully dusted. It was a great black thing with glass windows and monster black wheels. The Montana winged horse was emblazoned in a green shield on its heavy doors.

The rain continued to pour down. Paolo, who hated rain as much as the cats did, was glad the coach was real. The horses were not. They were four white cardboard cut-outs of horses, which were kept leaning against the wall of the coach-house. They were an economical idea of Old Niccolo's father's. As he said, real horses ate and needed exercise and took up space the family could live in. The coachman was another cardboard cut-out – for much the same reasons – but he was kept inside the coach.

The boys were longing to watch the cardboard figures being brought to life, but they were snatched indoors by their mother. Elizabeth's hair was soaking from her shift on the bridge and she was yawning until her jaw creaked, but this did not prevent her doing a very thorough scrubbing, combing and dressing job on Paolo and Tonino. By the time they came down into the yard again, each with his hair scraped wet to his head and wearing uncomfortable broad white collars above their stiff Eton jackets, the spell was done. The spell-streamers had been carefully wound into the harness, and the coachman clothed in a paper coat covered with spells on the inside. Four glossy white horses were stamping as they were backed into their traces. The coachman was sitting on the box adjusting his leaf-green hat.

"Splendid!" said Old Niccolo, bustling out. He looked approvingly from the boys to the coach. "Get in, boys. Get in, Domenico. We have to pick up Umberto from the University."

Tonino said goodbye to Benvenuto and climbed into the coach. It smelt of mould, in spite of the dusting. He was glad his grandfather was so cheerful. In fact everyone seemed to be. The family cheered as the coach rumbled to the gateway, and Old Niccolo smiled and waved back. Perhaps, Tonino thought, something good was going to come from this visit to the Duke, and no one would be so worried after this.

The journey in the coach was splendid. Tonino had never felt so grand before. The coach rumbled and swayed. The hooves of the horses clattered over the cobbles just as if they were real, and people hurried respectfully out of their way. The coachman was as good as spells could make him. Though puddles dimpled along every street, the coach was hardly splashed when they drew up at the University, with loud shouts of "Whoa there!"

Uncle Umberto climbed in, wearing his red and gold Master's gown, as cheerful as Old Niccolo. "Morning, Tonino," he said to Paolo. "How's your cat? Morning," he said to Domenico. "I hear the Petrocchis beat you up." Domenico, who would have died sooner than insult even a Petrocchi, went redder than Uncle Umberto's gown and swallowed noisily. But Uncle Umberto never could remember which younger Montana was which. He was too learned. He looked at Tonino as if he was wondering who he was, and turned to Old Niccolo.

"The Petrocchis are sure to help," he said. "I had word from Chrestomanci."

"So did I," said Old Niccolo, but he sounded dubious.

The coach rumbled down the rainswept Corso and turned out across the New Bridge, where it rumbled even more loudly. Paolo and Tonino stared out of the rainy windows, too excited to speak. Beyond the swollen river, they clopped uphill, where cypresses bent and lashed in front of rich villas, and then among blurred old walls. Finally they rumbled under a great archway and made a crisp turn round the gigantic forecourt of the Palace.

In front of their own coach, another coach, looking like a toy under the huge marble front of the Palace, was just drawing up by the enormous marble porch. This carriage was black too, with crimson shields on its doors, in which ramped black leopards. They were too late to see the people getting out of it, but they gazed with irritated envy at the coach itself and the horses. The horses were black, beautiful slender creatures with arched necks.

"I think they're *real* horses," Paolo whispered to Tonino.

Tonino had no time to answer, because two footmen and a soldier sprang to open the carriage door and usher them down, and Paolo jumped down first. But after him, Old Niccolo and Uncle Umberto were rather slow getting down. Tonino had time to look out of the further window at the Petrocchi carriage moving away. As it turned, he distinctly saw the small crimson flutter of a spell-streamer under the harness of the nearest black horse.

So there! Tonino thought triumphantly. But he rather thought the Petrocchi coachman was real. He was a pale young man with reddish hair which did not match his cherry-coloured livery, and he had an intent, concentrating look as if it was not easy driving those unreal horses. That look was too human for a cardboard man.

When Tonino finally climbed down on Domenico's

nervous heels, he glanced up at their own coachman for comparison. He was efficient and jaunty. He touched a stiff hand to his green hat and stared straight ahead. No, the Petrocchi coachman was real all right, Tonino thought enviously.

Tonino forgot both coachmen as he and Paolo followed the others into the Palace. It was so grand, and so huge. They were taken through vast halls with shiny floors and gilded ceilings, which seemed to go on for miles. On either side of the long walls there were statues, or soldiers, or footmen, adding to the magnificence in rows. They felt so battered by all the grandeur that it was quite a relief when they were shown into a room only about the size of the Casa Montana yard. True, the floor was shiny and the ceiling painted to look like a sky full of wrestling angels, but the walls were hung with quite comfortable red cloth and there was a row of almost plain gilt chairs along each side.

Another party of people was shown into the room at the same time. Domenico took one look at them and turned his eyes instantly on the painted angels of the ceiling. Old Niccolo and Uncle Umberto behaved as if the people were not there at all. Paolo and Tonino tried to do the same, but they found it impossible.

So these were the Petrocchis, they thought, sneaking glances. There were only four of them, to their five. One up to the Montanas. And two of those were children. Clearly the Petrocchis had been as hard-pressed as the Montanas to come before the Duke with a decent party, and they had, in Paolo and Tonino's opinion, made a bad mistake in leaving one of their family outside with the coach.

They were not impressive. Their University representative was a frail old man, far older than Uncle Umberto, who seemed almost lost in his red and gold gown. The most impressive one was the leader of the party, who must be Old Guido himself. But he was not particularly old, like Old Niccolo, and though he wore the same sort of black frock-coat as Old Niccolo and carried the same sort of shiny hat, it looked odd on Old Guido because he had a bright red beard. His hair was rather long, crinkly and black. And though he stared ahead in a bleak, important way, it was hard to forget that his daughter had once accidentally turned him green.

The two children were both girls. Both had reddish hair. Both had prim, pointed faces. Both wore bright white stockings and severe black dresses and were clearly odious. The main difference between them was that the younger – who seemed about Tonino's age – had a large bulging forehead, which made her face even primmer than her sister's. It was possible that one of them was the famous Angelica, who had turned Old Guido green.

The boys stared at them, trying to decide which it might be, until they encountered the prim, derisive stare of the elder girl. It was clear she thought they looked ridiculous. But Paolo and Tonino knew they still looked smart – they felt so uncomfortable – so they took no notice.

After they had waited a while, both parties began to

talk quietly among themselves, as if the others were not there. Tonino murmured to Paolo, "Which one is Angelica?"

"I don't know," Paolo whispered.

"Didn't you see them at the Old Bridge then?"

"I didn't see any of them. They were all down the other—"

Part of the red hanging swung aside and a lady hurried in. "I'm so sorry," she said. "My husband has been delayed."

Everyone in the room bent their heads and murmured "Your Grace" because this was the Duchess. But Paolo and Tonino kept their eyes on her while they bent their heads, wanting to know what she was like. She had a stiff greyish dress on, which put them in mind of a statue of a saint, and her face might almost have been part of the same statue. It was a statue-pale face, almost waxy, as if the Duchess were carved out of slightly soapy marble. But Tonino was not sure the Duchess was really like a saint. Her eyebrows were set in a strong sarcastic arch, and her mouth was tight with what looked like impatience. For a second, Tonino thought he felt that impatience – and a number of other unsaintly feelings – pouring into the room from behind the Duchess's waxy mask like a strong rank smell.

The Duchess smiled at Old Niccolo. "Signor Niccolo Montana?" There was no scrap of impatience, only stateliness. Tonino thought to himself, I've been reading too many books. Rather ashamed, he watched Old Niccolo bow and introduce them all. The Duchess nodded graciously and turned to the Petrocchis. "Signor Guido Petrocchi?"

The red-bearded man bowed in a rough, brusque way. He was nothing like as courtly as Old Niccolo. "Your Grace. With me are my great-uncle Dr Luigi Petrocchi, my elder daughter Renata, and my younger daughter Angelica."

Paolo and Tonino stared at the younger girl, from her bulge of forehead to her thin white legs. So *this* was Angelica. She did not look capable of doing anything wrong, or interesting.

The Duchess said, "I believe you understand why—"

The red curtains were once more swept aside. A bulky excited-looking man raced in with his head down, and took the Duchess by one arm. "Lucrezia, you must come! The scenery looks a treat!"

The Duchess turned as a statue might turn, all one piece. Her eyebrows were very high and her mouth pinched. "My lord Duke!" she said freezingly.

Tonino stared at the bulky man. He was now wearing slightly shabby green velvet with big brass buttons. Otherwise, he was exactly the same as the big damp Mr Glister who had interrupted the Punch and Judy show that time. So he had been the Duke of Caprona after all! And he was not in the least put off by the Duchess's frigid look. "You must come and look!" he said, tugging at her arm, as excited as ever. He turned to the Montanas and the Petrocchis as if he expected them to help him pull the Duchess out of the room – and then seemed to realise that they were not courtiers. "Who are you?"

"These," said the Duchess – her eyebrows were still higher and her voice was strong with patience – "these are the Petrocchis and the Montanas awaiting your pleasure, my lord."

The Duke slapped a large, damp-looking hand to his shiny forehead. "Well I'm blessed! The people who make spells! I was thinking of sending for you. Have you come about this enchanter-fellow who's got his knife into Caprona?" he asked Old Niccolo.

"My lord!" said the Duchess, her face rigid.

But the Duke broke away from her, beaming and gleaming, and dived on the Petrocchis. He shook Old Guido's hand hugely, and then the girl Renata's. After that, he dived round and did the same to Old Niccolo and Paolo. Paolo had to rub his hand secretly on his trousers after he let go. He was wet. "And they say the young ones are as clever as the old ones," the Duke said happily. "Amazing families! Just the people I need for my play – my pantomime, you know. We're putting it on here for Christmas and I could do with some special effects."

The Duchess gave a sigh. Paolo looked at her rigid face and thought that it must be hard, dealing with someone like the Duke.

The Duke dived on Domenico. "Can you arrange for a flight of cupids blowing trumpets?" he asked him eagerly. Domenico swallowed and managed to whisper the word "illusion". "Oh good!" said the Duke, and dived at Angelica Petrocchi. "And you'll love my collection of Punch and Judys," he said. "I've got hundreds!"

"How nice," Angelica answered primly.

"My lord," said the Duchess, "these good people did not come here to discuss the theatre."

"Maybe, maybe," the Duke said, with an impatient, eager wave of his large hand. "But while they're here, I might as well ask them about that too. Mightn't I?" he said, diving at Old Niccolo.

Old Niccolo showed great presence of mind. He smiled. "Of course, Your Grace. No trouble at all. After we've discussed the State business we came for, we shall be happy to take orders for any stage effects you want."

"So will we," said Guido Petrocchi, with a sour glance at the air over Old Niccolo.

The Duchess smiled graciously at Old Niccolo for backing her up, which made Old Guido look sourer than ever, and fixed the Duke with a meaning look.

It seemed to get through to the Duke at last. "Yes, yes," he said. "Better get down to business. It's like this, you see—"

The Duchess interrupted, with a gentle fixed smile. "Refreshments are laid out in the small Conference Room. If you and the adults like to hold your discussion there, I will arrange something for the children here."

Guido Petrocchi saw a chance to get even with Old Niccolo. "Your Grace," he barked stiffly, "my daughters are as loyal to Caprona as the rest of my house. I have no secrets from them."

The Duke flashed him a glistening smile. "Quite right! But they won't be half as bored if they stay here, will they?"

Quite suddenly, everyone except Paolo and Tonino

and the two Petrocchi girls was crowding away through another door behind the red hangings. The Duke leaned back, beaming. "I tell you what," he said, "you must come to my pantomime, all of you. You'll love it! I'll send you tickets. Coming, Lucrezia."

The four children were left standing under the ceiling full of wrestling angels.

After a moment, the Petrocchi girls walked to the chairs against the wall and sat down. Paolo and Tonino looked at one another. They marched to the chairs on the opposite side of the room and sat down there. It seemed a safe distance. From there, the Petrocchi girls were dark blurs with thin white legs and foxy blobs for heads.

"I wish I'd brought my book," said Tonino.

They sat with their heels hooked into the rungs of their chairs, trying to feel patient. "I think the Duchess must be a saint," said Paolo, "to be so patient with the Duke."

Tonino was surprised Paolo should think that. He knew the Duke did not behave much like a duke should, while the Duchess was every inch a duchess. But he was not sure it was right, the way she let them know how patient she was being. "Mother dashes about like that," he said, "and Father doesn't mind. It stops him looking worried."

"Father's not a Duchess," said Paolo.

Tonino did not argue because, at that moment, two footmen appeared, pushing a most interesting trolley. Tonino's mouth fell open. He had never seen so many cakes together in his life before. Across the room, there were black gaps in the faces of the Petrocchi girls.

Evidently they had never seen so many cakes either. Tonino shut his mouth quickly and tried to look as if he saw such sights every day.

The footmen served the Petrocchi girls first. They were very cool and seemed to take hours choosing. When the trolley was finally wheeled across to Paolo and Tonino, they found it hard to seem as composed. There were twenty different kinds of cake. They took ten each, with greedy speed, so that they had one of every kind between them and could swap if necessary. When the trolley was wheeled away, Tonino just managed to spare a glance from his plate to see how the Petrocchis were doing. Each girl had her white knees hooked up to carry a plate big enough to hold ten cakes.

They were rich cakes. By the time Paolo reached the tenth, he was going slowly, wondering if he really cared for meringue as much as he had thought, and Tonino was only on his sixth. By the time Paolo had put his plate neatly under his chair and cleaned himself with his handkerchief, Tonino, sticky with jam, smeared with chocolate and cream and infested with crumbs, was still doggedly ploughing through his eighth. And this was the moment the Duchess chose to sit smiling down beside Paolo.

"I won't interrupt your brother," she said, laughing. "Tell me about yourself, Paolo." Paolo did not know what to answer. All he could think of was the mess Tonino looked. "For instance," the Duchess asked helpfully, "does spell-making come easily to you? Do you find it hard to learn?"

"Oh no, Your Grace," Paolo said proudly. "I learn very easily." Then he was afraid this might upset Tonino. He looked quickly at Tonino's pastry-plastered face and found Tonino staring gravely at the Duchess. Paolo felt ashamed and responsible. He wanted the Duchess to know that Tonino was not just a messy staring little boy. "Tonino learns slowly," he said, "but he reads all the time. He's read all the books in the Library. He's almost as learned as Uncle Umberto."

"How remarkable," smiled the Duchess.

There was just a trace of disbelief in the arch of her eyebrows. Tonino was so embarrassed that he took a big bite out of his ninth cake. It was a great pastry puff. The instant his mouth closed round it, Tonino knew that, if he opened his mouth again, even to breathe, pastry would blow out of it like a hailstorm, all over Paolo and the Duchess. He clamped his lips together and chewed valiantly.

And, to Paolo's embarrassment, he went on staring at the Duchess. He was wishing Benvenuto was there to tell him about the Duchess. She muddled him. As she bent smiling over Paolo, she did not look like the haughty, rigid lady who had been so patient with the Duke. And yet, perhaps because she was not being patient, Tonino felt the rank strength of the unsaintly thoughts behind her waxy smile, stronger than ever.

Paolo willed Tonino to stop chewing and goggling. But Tonino went on, and the disbelief in the Duchess's eyebrows was so obvious, that he blurted out, "And Tonino's the only one who can talk to Benvenuto. He's our boss cat, Your—" He remembered the Duchess did not like cats. "Er – you don't like cats, Your Grace."

The Duchess laughed. "But I don't mind hearing about them. What about Benvenuto?"

To Paolo's relief, Tonino turned his goggle eyes from the Duchess to him. So Paolo talked on. "You see, Your Grace, spells work much better and stronger if a cat's around, and particularly if Benvenuto is. Besides Benvenuto knows all sorts of things—"

He was interrupted by a thick noise from Tonino. Tonino was trying to speak without opening his mouth. It was clear there was going to be a pastry-storm any second. Paolo snatched out his jammy, creamy handkerchief and held it ready.

The Duchess stood up, rather hastily. "I think I'd better see how my other guests are getting on," she said, and went swiftly gliding across to the Petrocchi girls.

The Petrocchi girls, Paolo noticed resentfully, were ready to receive her. Their handkerchiefs had been busy while the Duchess talked to Paolo, and now their plates were neatly pushed under their chairs too. Each had left at least three cakes. This much encouraged Tonino. He was feeling rather unwell. He put the rest of the ninth cake back beside the tenth and laid the plate carefully on the next chair. By this time, he had managed to swallow his mouthful.

"You shouldn't have told her about Benvenuto," he said, hauling out his handkerchief. "He's a family secret."

"Then you should have said something yourself

instead of staring like a dummy," Paolo retorted. To his mortification both Petrocchi girls were talking merrily to the Duchess. The bulge-headed Angelica was laughing. It so annoyed Paolo that he said, "Look at the way those girls are sucking up to the Duchess!"

"I didn't do that," Tonino pointed out.

As Paolo wanted to say he wished Tonino had, he found himself unable to say anything at all. He sat sourly watching the Duchess talking to the girls across the room, until she got up and went gliding away. She remembered to smile and wave at Paolo and Tonino as she went. Paolo thought that was good of her, considering the asses they had made of themselves.

Very soon after that, the curtains swung aside and Old Niccolo came back, walking slowly beside Guido Petrocchi. After them came the two gowned great-uncles, and Domenico came after that. It was like a procession. Everyone looked straight ahead, and it was plain they had a lot on their minds. All four children stood up, brushed crumbs off, and followed the procession. Paolo found he was walking beside the elder girl, but he was careful not to look at her. In utter silence, they marched to the great Palace door, where the carriages were moving along to receive them.

The Petrocchi carriage came first, with its black horses patched and beaded with rain. Tonino took another look at its coachman, rather hoping he had made a mistake. It was still raining and the man's clothes were soaked. His red Petrocchi hair was brown with wet under his wet hat. He was shivering as he leant down, and there was a questioning look on his pale face, as if he was anxious to be told what the Duke had said. No, he was real all right. The Montana coachman behind stared into space, ignoring the rain and his passengers equally. Tonino felt that the Petrocchis had definitely come out best.

CHAPTER FOUR

✳

When the coach was moving, Old Niccolo leaned back and said, "Well, the Duke is very good-natured, I'll say that. Perhaps he's not such a fool as he seems."

Uncle Umberto answered, with deepest gloom, "When my father was a boy, *his* father went to the Palace once a week. He was received as a friend."

Domenico said timidly, "At least we sold some stage effects."

"That," said Uncle Umberto crushingly, "is just what I'm complaining of."

Tonino and Paolo looked from one to the other, wondering what had depressed them so.

Old Niccolo noticed them looking. "Guido Petrocchi

wished those disgusting daughters of his to be present while we conferred with the Duke," he said. "I shall not—"

"Oh good Lord!" muttered Uncle Umberto. "One doesn't listen to a Petrocchi."

"No, but one trusts one's grandsons," said Old Niccolo. "Boys, old Caprona's in a bad way, it seems. The States of Florence, Pisa and Siena have now united against her. The Duke suspects they are paying an enchanter to—"

"Huh!" said Uncle Umberto. "Paying the Petrocchis."

Domenico, who had been rendered surprisingly bold by something, said, "Uncle, I could *see* the Petrocchis were no more traitors than we are!"

Both old men turned to look at him. He crumpled.

"The fact is," Old Niccolo continued, "Caprona is not the great State she once was. There are many reasons, no doubt. But we know, and the Duke knows – even Domenico knows – that each year we set the usual charms for the defence of Caprona, and each year we set them stronger, and each year they have less effect. Something – or someone – is definitely sapping our strength. So the Duke asks what else we can do. And—"

Domenico interrupted with a squawk of laughter. "And we said we'd find the words to the *Angel of Caprona*!"

Paolo and Tonino expected Domenico to be crushed again, but the two old men simply looked gloomy. Their heads nodded mournfully. "But I don't understand," said Tonino. "The *Angel of Caprona*'s got words. We sing them at school."

"Hasn't your mother taught you—?" Old Niccolo

began angrily. "Ah, no. I forgot. Your mother is English."

"One more reason for careful marriages," Uncle Umberto said dismally.

By this time, what with the rain ceaselessly pattering down as well, both boys were thoroughly depressed and alarmed. Domenico seemed to find them funny. He gave another squawk of laughter.

"Be quiet," said Old Niccolo. "This is the last time I take you where brandy is served. No, boys, the *Angel* has not got the right words. The words you sing are a makeshift. Some people say that the glorious Angel took the words back to Heaven after the White Devil was vanquished, leaving only the tune. Or the words have been lost since. But everyone knows that Caprona cannot be truly great until the words are found."

"In other words," Uncle Umberto said irritably, "the *Angel of Caprona* is a spell like any other spell. And without the proper words, any spell is only at half force, even if it is of divine origin." He gathered up his gown as the coach jerked to a stop outside the University. "And we – like idiots – have pledged ourselves to complete what God left unfinished," he said. "The presumption of man!" He climbed out of the coach, calling to Old Niccolo, "I'll look in every manuscript I can think of. There must be a clue somewhere. Oh this confounded rain!"

The door slammed and the coach jerked on again.

Paolo asked, "Have the Petrocchis said they'll find the words too?"

Old Niccolo's mouth bunched angrily. "They have. And I should die of shame if they did it before we did.

I—" He stopped as the coach lurched round the corner into the Corso. It lurched again, and jerked. Sprays of water flew past the windows.

Domenico leaned forward. "Not driving so well, is he?"

"Quiet!" said Old Niccolo, and Paolo bit his tongue in a whole succession of jerks. Something was wrong. The coach was not making the right noise.

"I can't hear the horses' hooves," Tonino said, puzzled.

"I thought that was it!" Old Niccolo snapped. "It's the rain." He let down the window with a bang, bringing in a gust of watery wind, and, regardless of faces staring up at him from under wet umbrellas, he leaned out and bellowed the words of a spell. "And drive quickly, coachman! There," he said, as he pulled the window up again, "that should get us home before the horses turn to pulp. What a blessing this didn't happen before Umberto got out!"

The noise of the horses' hooves sounded again, clopping over the cobbles of the Corso. It seemed that the new spell was working. But, as they turned into the Via Cardinale, the noise changed to a spongy *thump-thump*, and when they came to the Via Magica the hooves made hardly a sound. And the lurching and jerking began again, worse than ever. As they turned to enter the gate of the Casa Montana, there came the most brutal jerk of all. The coach tipped forward, and there was a crash as the pole hit the cobbles. Paolo got his window open in time to see the limp paper figure of the coachman flop off the box into a puddle. Beyond him, two wet cardboard horses were draped over their traces.

"That spell," said Old Niccolo, "lasted for days in my grandfather's time."

"Do you mean it's that enchanter?" Paolo asked. "Is he spoiling all our spells?"

Old Niccolo stared at him, full-eyed, like a baby about to burst into tears. "No, lad. I fancy not. The truth is, the Casa Montana is in as bad a way as Caprona. The old virtue is fading. It has faded generation by generation, and now it is almost gone. I am ashamed that you should learn it like this. Let's get out, boys, and start dragging."

It was a wretched humiliation. Since the rest of the family were all either asleep or at work on the Old Bridge, there was no one to help them pull the coach through the gate. And Domenico was no use. He confessed afterwards that he could not remember getting home. They left him asleep in the coach and dragged it in, just the three of them. Even Benvenuto dashing through the rain did not cheer Tonino much.

"One consolation," panted their grandfather. "The rain. There is no one about to see Old Niccolo dragging his own coach."

Paolo and Tonino did not find much consolation in that. Now they understood the growing unease in the Casa, and it was not pleasant. They understood why everyone was so anxious about the Old Bridge, and so delighted when, just before Christmas, it was mended at last. They understood, too, the worry about a husband for Rosa. As soon as the bridge was repaired, everyone went back to discussing that. And Paolo and Tonino knew why everyone agreed that the young man Rosa must choose, must have, if he had nothing else, a strong talent for spells.

"To improve the breed, you mean?" said Rosa. She was very sarcastic and independent about it. "Very well, dear Uncle Lorenzo, I shall only fall in love with men who can make paper horses waterproof."

Uncle Lorenzo blushed angrily. The whole family felt humiliated by those horses. But Elizabeth was trying not to laugh. Elizabeth certainly encouraged Rosa in her independent attitude. Benvenuto informed Tonino it was the English way. Cats liked English people, he added.

"Have we really lost our virtue?" Tonino asked Benvenuto anxiously. He thought it was probably the explanation for his slowness.

Benvenuto said that he did not know what it was like in the old days, but he knew there was enough magic about now to make his coat spark. It seemed like a lot. But he sometimes wondered if it was being applied properly.

Around this time, twice as many newspapers found their way into the Casa. There were journals from Rome and magazines from Genoa and Milan, as well as the usual Caprona papers. Everyone read them eagerly and talked in mutters about the attitude of Florence, movements in Pisa and opinion hardening in Siena. Out of the worried murmurs, the word *War* began to sound, more and more frequently. And, instead of the usual Christmas songs, the only tune heard in the Casa Montana, night and day, was the *Angel of Caprona*.

The tune was sung in bass, tenor and soprano. It was played slowly on flutes, picked out on guitars and lilted on violins. Every one of the Montanas lived in hope that he or she would be the person to find the true words. Rinaldo had a new idea. He procured a drum and sat on the edge of his bed beating out the rhythm, until Aunt Francesca implored him to stop. And even that did not help. Not one of the Montanas could begin to set the right words to the tune. Antonio looked so worried that Paolo could scarcely bear to look at him.

With so much to worry about, it was hardly surprising that Paolo and Tonino looked forward daily to being invited to the Duke's pantomime. It was the one bright spot. But Antonio and Rinaldo went to the Palace – on foot – to deliver the special effects, and came back without a word of invitation. Christmas came. The entire Montana family went to church, in the beautiful marble-fronted Church of Sant' Angelo, and behaved with great devotion. Usually it was only Aunt Anna and Aunt Maria who were notably religious, but now everyone felt they had something to pray for. It was only when the time came to sing the *Angel of Caprona* that the Montana devotion slackened. An absent-minded look came over their faces, from Old Niccolo to the smallest cousin. They sang:

> *"Merrily his music ringing,*
> *See an Angel cometh singing,*
> *Words of peace and comfort bringing*
> *To Caprona's city fair.*

Victory that faileth never,
Friendship that no strife can sever,
Lasting strength and peace for ever,
       For Caprona's city fair.

See the Devil flee astounded!
In Caprona now is founded
Virtue strong and peace unbounded—
       In Caprona's city fair."

Every one of them was wondering what the real words were.

They came home for the family celebrations, and there was still no word from the Duke. Then Christmas was over. New Year drew on and passed too, and the boys were forced to realise that there would be no invitation after all. Each told himself he had *known* the Duke was like that. They did not speak of it to one another. But they were both bitterly disappointed.

They were roused from their gloom by Lucia racing along the gallery, screaming, "Come and look at Rosa's young man!"

"What?" said Antonio, raising his worried face from a book about the Angel of Caprona. "What? Nothing's decided yet."

Lucia leapt from foot to foot. She was pink with excitement. "Rosa's decided for herself! I knew she would. Come and see!"

Led by Lucia, Antonio, Paolo, Tonino and Benvenuto

raced along the gallery and down the stone stairs at the end. People and cats were streaming through the courtyard from all directions, hurrying to the room called the Saloon, beyond the dining room.

Rosa was standing near the windows, looking happy but defiant, with both hands clasped round the arm of an embarrassed-looking young man with ginger hair. A bright ring winked on Rosa's finger. Elizabeth was with them, looking as happy as Rosa and almost as defiant. When the young man saw the family streaming through the door and crowding towards him, his face became bright pink and his hand went up to loosen his smart tie. But, in spite of that, it was plain to everyone that, underneath, the young man was as happy as Rosa. And Rosa was so happy that she seemed to shine, like the Angel over the gate. This made everyone stare, marvelling. Which, of course, made the young man more embarrassed than ever.

Old Niccolo cleared his throat. "Now look here," he said. Then he stopped. This was Antonio's business. He looked at Antonio.

Paolo and Tonino noticed that their father looked at their mother first. Elizabeth's happy look seemed to reassure him a little. "Now, just who are you?" he said to the young man. "How did you meet my Rosa?"

"He was one of the contractors on the Old Bridge, Father," said Rosa.

"And he has enormous natural talent, Antonio," said Elizabeth, "and a beautiful singing voice."

"All right, all right," said Antonio. "Let the boy speak for himself, women."

The young man swallowed, and helped the swallow down with a shake of his tie. His face was now very pale. "My name is Marco Andretti," he said in a pleasant, if husky, voice. "I – I think you met my brother at the bridge, sir. I was on the other shift. That's how I came to meet Rosa." The way he smiled down at Rosa left everybody hoping that he would be fit to become a Montana.

"It'll break their hearts if Father says no," Lucia whispered to Paolo. Paolo nodded. He could see that.

Antonio was pulling his lip, which was a thing he did when his face could hold no more worry than it did already.

"Yes," he said. "I've met Mario Andretti, of course. A very respectable family." He made that sound not altogether a good thing. "But I'm sure you're aware, Signor Andretti, that ours is a special family. We have to be careful who we marry. First, what do you think of the Petrocchis?"

Marco's pale face went fiery red. He answered with a violence which surprised the Montanas, "I hate their guts, Signor Montana!"

He seemed so upset that Rosa pulled his arm down and patted it soothingly.

"Marco has personal family reasons, Father," she said.

"Which I'd prefer not to go into," Marco said.

"We – well, I'll not press you for them," Antonio said, and continued to pull his lip. "But, you see, our family must marry someone with at least some talent for magic. Have you any ability there, Signor Andretti?"

Marco Andretti seemed to relax at this. He smiled, and gently took Rosa's hands off his sleeve. Then he sang. Elizabeth had been right about his voice. It was a golden tenor. Uncle Lorenzo was heard to rumble that he could not think what a voice like that was doing outside the Milan Opera.

> *"A golden tree there grows, a tree*
> *Whose golden branches bud with green..."*

sang Marco. As he sang, the tree came into being, rooted in the carpet between Rosa and Antonio, first as a faint gold shadow, then as a rattling metal shape, dazzling gold in the shafts of sunlight from the windows. The Montanas nodded their appreciation. The trunk and each branch, even the smallest twig, was indeed pure gold.

But Marco sang on, and as he sang, the gold twigs put out buds, pale and fist-shaped at first, then bright and pointed. Instants later, the tree was in leaf. It was moving and rattling constantly to Marco's singing. It put out pink and white flowers in clusters, which budded, expanded and dropped, as quickly as flames in a firework. The room was full of scent, then of petals fluttering like confetti. Marco still sang, and the tree still moved. Before the last petal had fallen, pointed green fruit was swelling where the flowers had been. The fruit grew brownish and swelled, and swelled and turned bulging and yellow, until the tree drooped under the weight of a heavy crop of big yellow pears.

"...With golden fruit for everyone,"

Marco concluded. He put up a hand, picked one of the pears and held it, rather diffidently, out to Antonio.

There were murmurs of appreciation from the rest of the family. Antonio took the pear and sniffed it. And he smiled, to Marco's evident relief. "Good fruit," he said. "That was very elegantly done, Signor Andretti. But there is one more thing I must ask you. Would you agree to change your name to Montana? That is our custom, you see."

"Yes, Rosa told me," said Marco. "And – and this is a difficulty. My brother needs me in his firm, and he too wants to keep his family name. Would it be all right if I'm known as Montana when I'm here, and as – as Andretti when I'm at home with my brother?"

"You mean you and Rosa wouldn't live here?" Antonio asked, astonished.

"Not all the time. No," said Marco. From the way he said it, it was clear he was not going to change his mind.

This was serious. Antonio looked at Old Niccolo. And there were grave faces all round at the thought of the family being broken up.

"I don't see why they shouldn't," said Elizabeth.

"Well – my great-uncle did it," Old Niccolo said. "But it was not a success. His wife ran off to Sicily with a greasy little warlock."

"That doesn't mean *I'm* going to!" Rosa said.

The family wavered, with the tree gently rattling in their midst. Everyone loved Rosa. Marco was clearly nice.

Nobody wanted to break their hearts. But this idea of living away from the Casa—!

Aunt Francesca heaved herself forward, saying, "I side with Elizabeth. Our Rosa has found herself a nice boy with more talent and a better voice than I've seen outside our family for years. Let them get married."

Antonio looked dreadfully worried at this, but he did not pull his lip. He seemed to be relaxing, ready to agree, when Rinaldo set the tree rattling furiously by pushing his way underneath it.

"Just a moment. Aren't we all being a bit trustful? Who *is* this fellow, after all? Why haven't we come across him and his talents before?"

Paolo hung his head and watched Rinaldo under his hair. This was Rinaldo in the mood he least admired. Rinaldo loud and aggressive, with an unpleasant twist to his mouth. Rinaldo was still a little pale from the cut on his head, but this went rather well with the black clothes and the red brigand's scarf. Rinaldo knew it did. He flung up his head with an air, and contemptuously brushed off a petal that had fallen on his black sleeve. And he looked at Marco, challenging him to answer.

The way Marco looked back showed that he was quite ready to stand up to Rinaldo. "I've been at college in Rome until recently," he said. "If that's what you mean."

Rinaldo swung round to face the family. "So he says," he said. "He's done a pretty trick for us, and said all the right things – but so would anyone in his place." He swung round on Marco. It was so dramatic that Tonino winced and even Paolo felt a little unhappy. "I don't trust you," said Rinaldo. "I've seen your face before somewhere."

"At the Old Bridge," said Marco.

"No, not there. It was somewhere else," said Rinaldo.

And this must be true, Tonino realised. Marco did have a familiar look. And Tonino could not have seen him at the Old Bridge, because Tonino had never been there.

"Do you want me to fetch my brother, or my priest, to vouch for me?" asked Marco.

"No," said Rinaldo rudely. "I want the truth."

Marco took a deep breath. "I don't want to be unfriendly," he said. The arm Rosa was not holding bent, and so did the fist on the end of it. Rinaldo gave it a look as if he welcomed it, and swaggered a step nearer.

"Please!" Rosa said uselessly.

Benvenuto moved in Tonino's arms. Into Tonino's head came a picture of a large stripy tomcat swaggering on the Casa roof – Benvenuto's roof. Tonino nearly laughed. Benvenuto's muscular back legs pushed him backwards into Paolo as Benvenuto took off. Benvenuto landed between Rinaldo and Marco. There was a gentle "Ah!" from the rest of the family. They knew Benvenuto would settle it.

Benvenuto deliberately ignored Rinaldo. Arching himself tall, with his tail straight up like a cypress tree, he minced to Marco's legs and rubbed himself round them. Marco undoubled his fist and bent to hold his hand out to Benvenuto. "Hallo," he said. "What's your name?" He paused, for Benvenuto to tell him. "I'm pleased to meet you, Benvenuto," he said.

The "Ah!" from the family was loud and long this time. It was followed by cries of, "Get out of it, Rinaldo! Don't make a fool of yourself! Leave Marco alone!"

Though Rinaldo was nothing like as easily crushed as Domenico, even he could not stand up to the whole family. When he looked at Old Niccolo and saw Old Niccolo waving him angrily aside, he gave up and shoved his way out of the room.

"Rosa and Marco," said Antonio, "I give my provisional consent to your marriage."

Upon that, everyone hugged everyone else, shook hands with Marco and kissed Rosa. Very flushed and happy, Marco plucked pear after pear from the golden tree and gave them to everyone, even the newest baby. They were delicious pears, ripe to perfection. They melted in mouths and dribbled down chins.

"I don't want to be a spoilsport," Aunt Maria said, slurping juice in Paolo's ear, "but a tree in the Saloon is going to be a nuisance."

But Marco had thought of that. As soon as the last pear was picked, the tree began to fade. Soon it was a clattering golden glitter, a vanishing shadow-tree, and then it was not there at all. Everyone applauded. Aunt Gina and Aunt Anna fetched bottles of wine and glasses, and the Casa drank to the health of Rosa and Marco.

"Thank goodness!" Tonino heard Elizabeth say. "I was so nervous for her!"

On the other side of Elizabeth, Old Niccolo was telling Uncle Lorenzo that Marco was a real acquisition, because he could understand cats. Tonino felt a little wistful at this. He went outside into the chilly yard. As he had expected, Benvenuto was now curled up in the sunny patch on the gallery steps. He undulated his tail in annoyance at Tonino. He had just settled down for a sleep.

But Marco could *not* understand cats, Benvenuto said irritably. He knew Benvenuto's name, because Rosa had told him, but he had no idea what Benvenuto had actually said to him. Benvenuto had told him that he and Rinaldo would get thoroughly scratched if they started a fight in the Casa – neither of them was boss cat here. Now, if Tonino would go away, a cat could get some sleep.

This was a great relief to Tonino. He now felt free to like Marco as much as Paolo did. Marco was fun. He was never in the Casa for very long, because he and his brother were building a villa out beyond the New Bridge, but he was one of the few people Tonino laid down his book to talk to. And that, Lucia told Rosa, was a compliment indeed.

Rosa and Marco were to be married in the spring. They laughed about it constantly as they swept in and out of the Casa together. Antonio and Uncle Lorenzo walked out to the villa where Mario Andretti lived, and arranged it all. Mario Andretti came to the Casa to settle the details. He was a large fat man – who drove a shrewd bargain, Aunt Francesca said – and quite different from Marco. The most notable thing about him was the long white motor car he came in.

Old Niccolo looked at that car reflectively. "It smells," he said. "But it looks more reliable than a cardboard horse." He sighed. He still felt deeply humiliated. All the same, after Mario Andretti had driven away, Tonino was very interested to be sent out to the post with two letters. One was addressed to Ferrari, the other to Rolls-Royce in England.

In the normal way, the talk in the Casa would have been all about that car and those two letters. But they passed unnoticed in the anxious murmurs about Florence, Siena and Pisa. The only topic able to drown out the talk of war was Rosa's wedding dress. Should it be long or short? With a train, or not? And what kind of veil? Rosa was quite as independent about that as she had been over Marco.

"I suppose I have no say in it at all," she said. "I shall have it knee-length one side and a train ten feet long on the other, I think. And no veil. Just a black mask."

This thoroughly offended Aunt Maria and Aunt Gina, who were the chief arguers. What with the noise they made, and the twanging the other side of the room, where Antonio had roped Marco in to help find the words to the *Angel*, Tonino was unable to concentrate on his book. He took it along the gallery to the library, hoping for peace there.

But Rinaldo was leaning on the gallery rail outside the library, looking remarkably sinister, and he stopped Tonino. "That Marco," he said. "I *wish* I could remember where I saw him. I've seen him in the Art Gallery with Rosa, but it wasn't there. I know it was somewhere much more damaging than that."

Tonino had no doubt that Rinaldo knew all sorts of damaging places. He took his book into the library, hoping that Rinaldo would not remember the place, and settled down in the chilly mustiness to read.

The next moment, Benvenuto landed on his book with a thump.

"Oh get off!" said Tonino. "I start school tomorrow, and I want to finish this first."

No, said Benvenuto. Tonino was to go to Old Niccolo *at once*. A flurry of scrips, spells, yellow parchment rolls and then a row of huge red books passed behind Tonino's eyes. It was followed by a storm of enormous images. Giants were running, banging, smoking and burning, and they all wore red and gold. But not yet. They were preparing to fight, marching in great huge boots. Benvenuto was so urgent that it took all Tonino's skill to sort out what he meant.

"All right," said Tonino. "I'll tell him." He got up and pelted round the gallery, past Rinaldo, who said, "What's the hurry?" to Old Niccolo's quarters. Old Niccolo was just coming out.

"Please," said Tonino, "Benvenuto says to get out the war-spells. The Duke is calling up the Reserves."

Old Niccolo stood so very quiet and wide-eyed that Tonino thought he did not believe it. Old Niccolo was feeling for the door-frame. He seemed to think it was missing.

"You did hear me, did you?" Tonino asked.

"Yes," said Old Niccolo. "Yes, I heard. It's just so soon – so sudden. I wish the Duke had warned us. So war is coming. Pray God our strength is still enough."

Chapter Five

*

*B*envenuto's news caused a stampede in the Casa Montana. The older cousins raced to the Scriptorium and began packing away all the usual spells, inks and pens. The aunts fetched out the special inks for use in war-spells. The uncles staggered under reams of fresh paper and parchment. Antonio, Old Niccolo and Rinaldo went to the library and fetched the giant red volumes, with *WAR* stamped on their spines, while Elizabeth raced to the music room with all the children to put away the ordinary music and set out the tunes and instruments of war.

Meanwhile, Rosa, Marco and Domenico raced out into the Via Magica and came back with newspapers. Everyone at once left what they were doing and crowded into the dining room to see what the papers said.

They made a pile of people, all craning over the table. Rinaldo was standing on a chair, leaning over three aunts. Marco was underneath, craning anxiously sideways, head to head with Old Niccolo, as Rosa flipped over the pages. There were so many other people packed in and leaning over that Lucia, Paolo and Tonino were forced to squat with their chins on the table, in order to see at all.

"No, nothing," Rosa said, flipping over the second paper.

"Wait," said Marco. "Look at the Stop Press."

Everyone swayed towards it, pushing Marco further sideways. Then Tonino almost knew where he had seen Marco before.

"There it is," said Antonio.

All the bodies came upright, with their faces very serious.

"Reserve mobilised, right enough," said Rosa. "Oh, Marco!"

"What's the matter?" Rinaldo asked jeeringly from his chair. "Is Marco a Reservist?"

"No," said Marco. "My – my brother got me out of it."

Rinaldo laughed. "What a patriot!"

Marco looked up at him. "I'm a Final Reservist," he said, "and I hope you are too. If you aren't, it will be a pleasure to take you round to the Army Office in the Arsenal this moment."

The two glared at one another. Once again there were shouts to Rinaldo to stop making a fool of himself. Sulkily, Rinaldo climbed down and stalked out.

"Rinaldo *is* a Final Reservist," Paolo assured Marco.

"I thought he must be," Marco said. "Look, I must go. I – I must tell my brother. Rosa, I'll see you tomorrow if I can."

When Tonino fell asleep that night, the room next door to him was full of people talking of war and the *Angel of Caprona*, with occasional digressions about Rosa's wedding dress. Tonino's head was so full of these things that he was quite surprised, when he went to school, not to hear them talked of there. But no one seemed to have noticed there might be a war. True, some of the teachers looked grave, but that might have been just their natural feelings at the start of a new term.

Consequently, Tonino came home that afternoon thinking that maybe things were not so bad after all. As usual, Benvenuto leapt off the water butt and sprang into his arms. Tonino was rubbing his face against Benvenuto's nearest ragged ear, when he heard a carriage draw up behind him. Benvenuto promptly squirmed out of Tonino's arms. Tonino, very surprised, looked round to find him trotting, gently and politely, with his tail well up, towards a tall man who was just coming in through the Casa gate.

Benvenuto stood, his brush of tail waving slightly at the tip, his hind legs canted slightly apart under his fluffy drawers, staring gravely at the tall man. Tonino thought peevishly that, from behind, Benvenuto often looked pretty silly. The man looked almost as bad. He was wearing an exceedingly expensive coat with a fur collar and a tweed travelling cap with daft earflaps. And he bowed to Benvenuto.

"Good afternoon, Benvenuto," he said, as grave as Benvenuto himself. "I'm glad to see you so well. Yes, I'm very well thank you."

Benvenuto advanced to rub himself round the stranger's legs.

"No," said the man. "I beg you. Your hairs come off."

And Benvenuto stopped, without abating an ounce of his uncommon politeness.

By this time, Tonino was extremely resentful. This was the first time for years that Benvenuto had behaved as if anyone mattered more than Tonino. He raised his eyes accusingly to the stranger's. He met eyes even darker than his own, which seemed to spill brilliance over the rest of the man's smooth dark face. They gave Tonino a jolt, worse than the time the horses turned back to cardboard. He knew, beyond a shadow of doubt, that he was looking at a powerful enchanter.

"How do you do?" said the man. "No, despite your accusing glare, young man, I have never been able to understand cats – or not more than in the most general way. I wonder if you would be kind enough to translate for me what Benvenuto is saying."

Tonino listened to Benvenuto. "He says he's very pleased to see you again and welcome to the Casa Montana, sir." The *sir* was from Benvenuto, not Tonino. Tonino was not sure he cared for strange enchanters who walked into the Casa and took up Benvenuto's attention.

"Thank you, Benvenuto," said the enchanter. "I'm very pleased to be back. Though, frankly, I've seldom had such a difficult journey. Did you know your borders with

Florence and Pisa were closed?" he asked Tonino. "I had to come in by sea from Genoa in the end."

"Did you?" Tonino said, wondering if the man thought it was his fault. "Where did you come from then?"

"Oh, England," said the man.

Tonino warmed to that. This then could not be the enchanter the Duke had talked about. Or could he? Tonino was not sure how far away enchanters could work from.

"Makes you feel better?" asked the man.

"Mother's English," Tonino admitted, feeling he was giving altogether too much away.

"Ah!" said the enchanter. "Now I know who you are. You're Antonio the Younger, aren't you? You were a baby when I saw you last, Tonino."

Since there is no reply to that kind of remark, Tonino was glad to see Old Niccolo hastening across the yard, followed by Aunt Francesca and Uncle Lorenzo, with Antonio and several more of the family hurrying behind them. They closed round the enchanter, leaving Tonino and Benvenuto beyond, by the gate.

"Yes, I've just come from the Casa Petrocchi," Tonino heard the stranger say. To his surprise, everyone accepted it, as if it were the most natural thing for the stranger to have done – as natural as the way he took off his ridiculous English hat to Aunt Francesca.

"But you'll stay the night with us," said Aunt Francesca.

"If it's not too much trouble," the stranger said.

In the distance, as if they already knew – as they unquestionably did in a place like the Casa Montana – Aunt Maria and Aunt Anna went clambering up the gallery steps to prepare the guest room above. Aunt Gina emerged from the kitchen, held her hands up to Heaven, and dashed indoors again. Thoughtfully, Tonino gathered up Benvenuto and asked exactly who this stranger was.

Chrestomanci, of course, he was told. The most powerful enchanter in the world.

"Is he the one who's spoiling our spells?" Tonino asked suspiciously.

Chrestomanci, he was told – impatiently, because Benvenuto evidently thought Tonino was being very stupid – is always on our side.

Tonino looked at the stranger again – or rather, at his smooth dark head sticking out from among the shorter Montanas – and understood that Chrestomanci's coming meant there was a crisis indeed.

The stranger must have said something about him. Tonino found them all looking at him, his family smiling lovingly. He smiled back shyly.

"Oh, he's a good boy," said Aunt Francesca.

Then they all surged, talking, across the yard. "What makes it particularly difficult," Tonino heard Chrestomanci saying, "is that I am, first and foremost, an employee of the British Government. And Britain is keeping out of Italian affairs. But luckily I have a fairly wide brief."

Almost at once, Aunt Gina shot out of the kitchen again. She had cancelled the ordinary supper and started on a new one in honour of Chrestomanci. Six people were sent out at once for cakes and fruit, and two more for lettuce and cheese. Paolo, Corinna and Lucia were caught as they came in chatting from school and told to go at once to the butcher's. But, at this point, Rinaldo erupted furiously from the Scriptorium.

"What do you mean, sending all the kids off like this!" he bawled from the gallery. "We're up to our ears in war-spells here. I need copiers!"

Aunt Gina put her hands on her hips and bawled back at him. "And I need steak! Don't you stand up there cheeking me, Rinaldo Montana! English people always eat steak, so steak I must have!"

"Then cut pieces off the cats!" screamed Rinaldo. "I need Corinna and Lucia up here!"

"I tell you they are going to run after *me* for once!" yelled Aunt Gina.

"Dear me," said Chrestomanci, wandering into the yard. "What a very Italian scene! Can I help in any way?" He nodded and smiled from Aunt Gina to Rinaldo. Both of them smiled back, Rinaldo at his most charming.

"You would agree I need copiers, sir, wouldn't you?" he said.

"Bah!" said Aunt Gina. "Rinaldo turns on the charm and I get left to struggle alone! As usual! All right. Because it's war-spells, Paolo and Tonino can go for the steak. But wait while I write you a note, or you'll come back with something no one can chew."

"So glad to be of service," Chrestomanci murmured, and turned away to greet Elizabeth, who came racing down from the gallery waving a sheaf of music and fell into his arms. The heads of the five little cousins Elizabeth had been teaching stared wonderingly over the gallery rail. "Elizabeth!" said Chrestomanci. "Looking younger than ever!" Tonino stared as wonderingly as his cousins. His mother was laughing and crying at once. He could not follow the torrent of English speech. "Virtue," he heard, and "war" and, before long, the inevitable "*Angel of Caprona*". He was still staring when Aunt Gina stuck her note into his hand and told him to make haste.

As they hurried to the butcher's, Tonino said to Paolo, "I didn't know Mother knew anyone like Chrestomanci."

"Neither did I," Paolo confessed. He was only a year older than Tonino, after all, and it seemed that Chrestomanci had last been in Caprona a very long time ago. "Perhaps he's come to find the words to the *Angel*," Paolo suggested. "I hope so. I don't want Rinaldo to have to go away and fight."

"Or Marco," Tonino agreed. "Or Carlo or Luigi or even Domenico."

Because of Aunt Gina's note, the butcher treated them with great respect. "Tell her this is the last good steak she'll see, if war is declared," he said, and he passed them each a heavy, squashy pink armload.

They arrived back with their armfuls just as a cab set down Uncle Umberto, puffing and panting, outside the Casa gate. "I am right, Chrestomanci *is* here? Eh, Paolo?" Uncle Umberto asked Tonino.

Both boys nodded. It seemed easier than explaining that Paolo was Tonino.

"Good, good!" exclaimed Uncle Umberto and surged into the Casa, where he found Chrestomanci just crossing the yard. "The *Angel of Caprona*," Uncle Umberto said to him eagerly. "Could you—?"

"My dear Umberto," said Chrestomanci, shaking his hand warmly, "everyone here is asking me that. For that matter, so was everyone in the Casa Petrocchi too. And I'm afraid I know no more than you do. But I shall think about it, don't worry."

"If you could find just a line, to get us started," Uncle Umberto said pleadingly.

"I *will* do my best!" Chrestomanci was saying, when, with a great clattering of heels, Rosa shot past. From the look on her face, she had seen Marco arriving. "I promise you that," Chrestomanci said, as his head turned to see what Rosa was running for.

Marco came through the gate and stopped so dead, staring at Chrestomanci, that Rosa charged into him and nearly knocked him over. Marco staggered a bit, put his arms round Rosa, and went on staring at Chrestomanci. Tonino found himself holding his breath. Rinaldo was right. There *was* something about Marco. Chrestomanci knew it, and Marco knew he knew. From the look on Marco's face, he expected Chrestomanci to say what it was.

Chrestomanci indeed opened his mouth to say something, but he shut it again and pursed his lips in a sort of whistle instead. Marco looked at him uncertainly.

"Oh," said Uncle Umberto, "may I introduce—" He stopped and thought. Rosa he usually remembered, because of her fair hair, but he could not place Marco. "Corinna's fiancé," he suggested.

"I'm Rosa," said Rosa. "This is Marco Andretti."

"How do you do?" Chrestomanci said politely. Marco seemed to relax. Chrestomanci's eyes turned to Paolo and Tonino, standing staring. "Good heavens!" he said. "Everyone here seems to live such exciting lives. What have you boys killed?"

Paolo and Tonino looked down in consternation, to find that the steak was leaking on to their shoes. Two or three cats were approaching meaningly.

Aunt Gina appeared in the kitchen doorway. "*Where's my steak?*"

Paolo and Tonino sped towards her, leaving a pattering trail. "What was all that about?" Paolo panted to Tonino.

"I don't know," said Tonino, because he didn't, and because he liked Marco.

Aunt Gina shortly became very sharp and passionate about the steak. The leaking trail attracted every cat in the Casa. They were underfoot in the kitchen all evening, mewing pitifully. Benvenuto was also present, at a wary distance from Aunt Gina, and he made good use of his time. Aunt Gina erupted into the yard again, trumpeting.

"Tonino! *Ton-in-ooh!*"

Tonino laid down his book and hurried outside. "Yes, Aunt Gina?"

"That cat of yours has stolen a whole pound of steak!" Aunt Gina trumpeted, flinging a dramatic arm skyward.

Tonino looked, and there, sure enough, Benvenuto was, crouched on the pantiles of the roof, with one paw holding down quite a large lump of meat. "Oh dear," he said. "I don't think I can make him give it back, Aunt Gina."

"I don't want it back. Look where it's been!" screamed Aunt Gina. "Tell him from me that I shall wring his evil neck if he comes near me again!"

"My goodness, you do seem to be at the centre of everything," Chrestomanci remarked, appearing beside Tonino in the yard. "Are you always in such demand?"

"I shall have hysterics," declared Aunt Gina. "And no one will get any supper."

Elizabeth and Aunt Maria and Cousins Claudia and Teresa immediately came to her assistance and led her tenderly back indoors.

"Thank the Lord!" said Chrestomanci. "I'm not sure I could stand hysterics and starvation at once. How did you know I was an enchanter, Tonino? From Benvenuto?"

"No. I just knew when I looked at you," said Tonino.

"I see," said Chrestomanci. "This is interesting. Most people find it impossible to tell. It makes me wonder if Old Niccolo is right, when he talks of the virtue leaving your house. Would you be able to tell another enchanter when you looked at him, do you think?"

Tonino screwed up his face and wondered. "I might. It's the eyes. You mean, would I know the enchanter who's spoiling our spells?"

"I think I mean that," said Chrestomanci. "I'm beginning to believe there is someone. I'm sure, at least, that the spells on the Old Bridge were deliberately broken. Would it interfere with your plans too much, if I asked your grandfather to take you with him whenever he has to meet strangers?"

"I haven't got any plans," said Tonino. Then he thought, and he laughed. "I think you make jokes all the time."

"I aim to please," Chrestomanci said.

However, when Tonino next saw Chrestomanci, it was at supper – which was magnificent, despite Benvenuto and the hysterics – and Chrestomanci was very serious indeed. "My dear Niccolo," he said, "my mission *has* to concern the misuse of magic, not the balance of power in Italy. There would be no end of trouble if I was caught trying to stop a war."

Old Niccolo had his look of a baby about to cry. Aunt Francesca said, "We're not asking this personally—"

"But, my dear," said Chrestomanci, "don't you see that I can only do something like this as a personal matter? Please ask me personally. I shan't let the strict terms of my mission interfere with what I owe my friends." He smiled then, and his eyes swept round everyone gathered at the great table, very affectionately. He did not seem to exclude Marco. "So," he said, "I think my best plan for the moment is to go on to Rome. I know certain quarters there, where I can get impartial information, which should enable me to pin down this enchanter. At the moment, all we know is that he exists. If I'm lucky, I can prove whether Florence, or Siena, or Pisa is paying him – in which case, they and he can be indicted at the Court of Europe. And if, while I'm at it, I can get Rome, or Naples, to move on Caprona's behalf, be very sure I shall do it."

"Thank you," said Old Niccolo.

For the rest of supper, they discussed how Chrestomanci could best get to Rome. He would have to go by sea. It seemed that the last stretch of border, between Caprona and Siena, was now closed.

Much later that night, when Paolo and Tonino were on their way to bed, they saw lights in the Scriptorium. They tiptoed along to investigate. Chrestomanci was there with Antonio, Rinaldo and Aunt Francesca, going through spells in the big red books. Everyone was speaking in mutters, but they heard Chrestomanci say, "This is a sound combination, but it'll need new words." And on another page, "Get Elizabeth to put this in English, as a surprise factor." And again, "Ignore the tune. The only tune which is going to be any use to you at the moment is the *Angel*. He can't block that."

"Why just those three?" Tonino whispered.

"They're best at making new spells," Paolo whispered back. "We need new war-spells. It sounds as if the other enchanter knows the old ones."

They crept to bed with an excited, urgent feeling, and neither of them found it easy to sleep.

Chrestomanci left the next morning before the children went to school. Benvenuto and Old Niccolo escorted him to the gate, one on either side, and the entire Casa gathered to wave him off. Things felt both flat and worrying once he was gone. That day, there was a great deal of talk of war at school. The teachers whispered together. Two had left, to join the Reserves. Rumours went round the classes. Someone told Tonino that war would be declared next Sunday, so that it would be a Holy War.

Someone else told Paolo that all the Reserves had been issued with two left boots, so that they would not be able to fight. There was no truth in these things. It was just that everyone now knew that war was coming.

The boys hurried home, anxious for some real news. As usual, Benvenuto leapt off his water butt. While Tonino was enjoying Benvenuto's undivided attention again, Elizabeth called from the gallery, "Tonino! Someone's sent you a parcel."

Tonino and Benvenuto sprang for the gallery stairs, highly excited. Tonino had never had a parcel before. But before he got anywhere near it, he was seized on by Aunt Maria, Rosa and Uncle Lorenzo. They seized on all the children who could write and hurried them to the dining room. This had been set up as another Scriptorium. By each chair was a special pen, a bottle of red war-ink and a pile of strips of paper. There the children were kept busy fully two hours, copying the same war-charm, again and again. Tonino had never been so frustrated in his life. He did not even know what shape his parcel was. He was not the only one to feel frustrated.

"Oh, why?" complained Lucia, Paolo and young Cousin Lena.

"I know," said Aunt Maria. "Like school again. Start writing."

"It's exploiting children, that's what we're doing," Rosa said cheerfully. "There are probably laws against it, so do complain."

"Don't worry, I will," said Lucia. "I am doing."

"As long as you write while you grumble," said Rosa.

"It's a new spell-scrip for the Army," Uncle Lorenzo explained. "It's very urgent."

"It's hard. It's all new words," Paolo grumbled.

"Your father made it last night," said Aunt Maria. "Get writing. We'll be watching for mistakes."

When finally, stiff-necked and with red splodges on their fingers, they were let out into the yard, Tonino discovered that he had barely time to unwrap the parcel before supper. Supper was early that night, so that the elder Montanas could put in another shift on the army-spells before bedtime.

"It's worse than working on the Old Bridge," said Lucia. "What's that, Tonino? Who sent it?"

The parcel was promisingly book-shaped. It bore the stamp and the arms of the University of Caprona. This was the only indication Tonino had that Uncle Umberto had sent it, for, when he wrenched off the thick brown paper, there was no letter, not even a card. There was only a new shiny book. Tonino's face beamed. At least Uncle Umberto knew this much about him. He turned the book lovingly over. It was called *The Boy Who Saved His Country*, and the cover was the same shiny, pimpled red leather as the great volumes of war-spells.

"Is Uncle Umberto trying to give you a hint, or something?" Paolo asked, amused. He and Lucia and Corinna leant over Tonino while he flipped through the pages. There were pictures, to Tonino's delight. Soldiers rode horses, soldiers rode machines; a boy hung from a rope and scrambled up the frowning wall of a fortress; and, most exciting of all, a boy stood on a rock with a flag, confronting a whole troop of ferocious-looking dragoons. Sighing with anticipation, Tonino turned to Chapter One: *How Giorgio Uncovered an Enemy Plot.*

"*Supper!*" howled Aunt Gina from the yard. "Oh I shall go mad! Nobody attends to me!"

Tonino was forced to shut the lovely book again and hurry down to the dining room. He watched Aunt Gina anxiously as she doled out minestrone. She looked so hectic that he was convinced Benvenuto must have been at work in the kitchen again.

"It's all right," Rosa said. "It's just she thought she'd got a line from the *Angel of Caprona*. Then the soup boiled over and she forgot it again."

Aunt Gina was distinctly tearful. "With so much to do, my memory is like a sieve," she kept saying. "Now I've let you all down."

"Of course you haven't, Gina my dear," said Old Niccolo. "This is nothing to worry about. It will come back to you."

"But I can't even remember what language it was in!" wailed Aunt Gina.

Everyone tried to console her. They sprinkled grated cheese on their soup and slurped it with special relish, to show Aunt Gina how much they appreciated her, but Aunt Gina continued to sniff and accuse herself. Then Rinaldo thought of pointing out that she had got further than anyone else in the Casa Montana. "None of the rest of us has any of the *Angel of Caprona* to forget," he said, giving Aunt Gina his best smile.

"Bah!" said Aunt Gina. "Turning on the charm,

Rinaldo Montana!" But she seemed a good deal more cheerful after that.

Tonino was glad Benvenuto had nothing to do with it this time. He looked round for Benvenuto. Benvenuto usually took up a good position for stealing scraps, near the serving table. But tonight he was nowhere to be seen. Nor, for that matter, was Marco.

"Where's Marco?" Paolo asked Rosa.

Rosa smiled. She seemed quite cheerful about it. "He has to help his brother," she said, "with fortifications."

That brought home to Paolo and Tonino the fact that there was going to be a war. They looked at one another nervously. Neither of them was quite sure whether you behaved in the usual way in wartime, or not. Tonino's mind shot to his beautiful new book, *The Boy Who Saved His Country*. He slurped the title through his mind, just as he was slurping his soup. Had Uncle Umberto meant to say to him, find the words to the *Angel of Caprona* and save your country, Tonino? It would indeed be the most marvellous thing if he, Tonino Montana, could find the words and save his country. He could hardly wait to see how the boy in the book had done it.

As soon as supper was over, he sprang up, ready to dash off and start reading. And once again he was prevented. This time it was because the children were told to wash up supper. Tonino groaned. And, again, he was not the only one.

"It isn't fair!" Corinna said passionately. "We slave all afternoon at spells, and we slave all evening at washing-up! I know there's going to be a war, but I still have to do my exams. How am I ever going to do my homework?" The way she flung out an impassioned arm made Paolo and Tonino think that Aunt Gina's manner must be catching.

Rather unexpectedly, Lucia sympathised with Corinna. "I think you're too old to be one of us children," she said. "Why don't you go away and do your homework and let me organise the kids?"

Corinna looked at her uncertainly. "What about your homework?"

"I've not got much. I'm not aiming for the University like you," Lucia said kindly. "Run along." And she pushed Corinna out of the dining room. As soon as the door was shut, she turned briskly to the other children. "Come on. What are you lot standing gooping for? Everyone take a pile of plates to the kitchen. Quick march, Tonino. Move, Lena and Bernardo. Paolo, you take the big bowls."

With Lucia standing over them like a sergeant major, Tonino had no chance to slip away. He trudged to the kitchen with everyone else, where, to his surprise, Lucia ordered everyone to lay the plates and cutlery out in rows on the floor. Then she made them stand in a row themselves, facing the rows of greasy dishes.

Lucia was very pleased with herself. "Now," she said, "this is something I've always wanted to try. This is washing-up-made-easy, by Lucia Montana's patent method. I'll tell you the words. They go to the *Angel of Caprona*. And you're all to sing after me—"

"Are you sure we should?" asked Lena, who was a very law-abiding cousin.

Lucia gave her a look of scalding contempt. "If some

people," she remarked to the whitewashed beams of the ceiling, "don't know true intelligence when they see it, they are quite at liberty to go and live with the Petrocchis."

"I only asked," Lena said, crushed.

"Well, don't," said Lucia. "This is the spell…"

Shortly, they were all singing lustily:

"Angel, clean our knives and dishes,
Clean our spoons and salad-bowls,
Wash our saucepans, hear our wishes,
Angel, make our forks quite clean."

At first, nothing seemed to happen. Then it became clear that the orange grease was certainly slowly clearing from the plates. Then the lengths of spaghetti stuck to the bottom of the largest saucepan started unwinding and wriggling like worms. Up over the edge of the saucepan they wriggled, and over the stone floor, to ooze themselves into the waste-cans. The orange grease and the salad oil travelled after them, in rivulets. And the singing faltered a little, as people broke off to laugh.

"Sing, *sing!*" shouted Lucia. So they sang.

Unfortunately for Lucia, the noise penetrated to the Scriptorium. The plates were still pale pink and rather greasy, and the last of the spaghetti was still wriggling across the floor, when Elizabeth and Aunt Maria burst into the kitchen.

"Lucia!" said Elizabeth.

"You irreligious brats!" said Aunt Maria.

"I don't see what's so wrong," said Lucia.

"She doesn't see – Elizabeth, words fail!" said Aunt Maria. "How can I have taught her so little and so badly? Lucia, a spell is not *instead* of a thing. It is only to *help* that thing. And on top of that, you go and use the *Angel of Caprona*, as if it was any old tune, and not the most powerful song in all Italy! I – I could box your ears, Lucia!"

"So could I," said Elizabeth. "Don't you understand we need all our virtue – the whole combined strength of the Casa Montana – to put into the war-charms? And here you go frittering it away in the kitchen!"

"Put those plates in the sink, Paolo," ordered Aunt Maria. "Tonino, pick up those saucepans. The rest of you pick up the cutlery. And now you'll wash them properly."

Very chastened, everyone obeyed. Lucia was angry as well as chastened. When Lena whispered, "I *told* you so!" Lucia broke a plate and jumped on the pieces.

"Lucia!" snapped Aunt Maria, glaring at her. It was the first time any of the children had seen her look likely to slap someone.

"Well, how was I to know?" Lucia stormed. "Nobody ever explained – nobody *told* me spells were like that!"

"Yes, but you knew perfectly well you were doing something you shouldn't," Elizabeth told her, "even if you didn't know why. The rest of you, stop sniggering. Lena, you can learn from this too."

All through doing the washing-up properly – which took nearly an hour – Tonino was saying to himself, "And *then* I can read my book at last."

When it was finally done, he sped out into the yard.

And there was Old Niccolo hurrying down the steps to meet him in the dark.

"Tonino, may I have Benvenuto for a while, please?"

But Benvenuto was still not to be found. Tonino began to think he would die of book-frustration. All the children joined in hunting and calling, but there was still no Benvenuto. Soon, most of the grown-ups were looking for him too, and still Benvenuto did not appear. Antonio was so exasperated that he seized Tonino's arm and shook him.

"It's too bad, Tonino! You must have known we'd need Benvenuto. Why did you let him go?"

"I didn't! You *know* what Benvenuto's like!" Tonino protested, equally exasperated.

"Now, now, now," said Old Niccolo, taking each of them by a shoulder. "It is quite plain by now that Benvenuto is on the other side of town, making vile noises on a roof somewhere. All we can do is hope someone empties a jug of water on him soon. It's not Tonino's fault, Antonio."

Antonio let go Tonino's arm and rubbed both hands on his face. He looked very tired. "I'm sorry, Tonino," he said. "Forgive me. Let us know as soon as Benvenuto comes back, won't you?"

He and Old Niccolo hurried back to the Scriptorium. As they passed under the light, their faces were stiff with worry. "I don't think I like war, Tonino," Paolo said. "Let's go and play table-tennis in the dining room."

"I'm going to read my book," Tonino said firmly. He thought he would get like Aunt Gina if anything else happened to stop him.

CHAPTER SIX

✳

*T*onino read half the night. With all the grown-ups hard at work in the Scriptorium, there was no one to tell him to go to bed. Corinna tried, when she had finished her homework, but Tonino was too deep in the book even to hear her. And Corinna went respectfully away, thinking that, as the book had come from Uncle Umberto, it was probably very learned.

It was not in the least learned. It was the most gripping story Tonino had ever read. It started with the boy, Giorgio, going along a mysterious alleyway near the docks on his way home from school. There was a peeling blue house at the end of the alley and, just as Giorgio passed it, a scrap of paper fluttered from one of its windows. It contained a mysterious message, which led Giorgio at once into a set of adventures with the enemies of his country. Each one was more exciting than the last.

Well after midnight, when Giorgio was holding a pass single-handed against the enemy, Tonino happened to hear his father and mother coming to bed. He was forced to leave Giorgio lying wounded and dive into bed himself. All night he dreamt of notes fluttering from the windows of peeling blue houses, of Giorgio – who was sometimes Tonino himself and sometimes Paolo – and of villainous enemies – most of whom seemed to have red beards and black hair, like Guido Petrocchi – and, as the sun rose, he was too excited to stay asleep. He woke up and went on reading.

When the rest of the Casa Montana began to stir, Tonino had finished the book. Giorgio had saved his country. Tonino was quivering with excitement and exhaustion. He wished the book was twice as long. If it had not been time to get up, he would have gone straight back to the beginning and started reading the book again.

And the beauty of it, he thought, eating breakfast without noticing, was that Giorgio had saved his country, not only single-handed, but without a spell coming into it anywhere. If Tonino was going to save Caprona, that was the way he would like to do it.

Around Tonino, everyone else was complaining and Lucia was sulking. The washing-up spell was still about in the kitchen. Every cup and plate was covered with a thin layer of orange spaghetti grease, and the butter tasted of soap.

"What did she *use*, in Heaven's name?" groaned Uncle Lorenzo. "This coffee tastes of tomato."

"Her own words to the *Angel of Caprona*," Aunt Maria said, and shuddered as she picked up her greasy cup.

"Lucia, you fool!" said Rinaldo. "That's the strongest tune there is."

"All right, all right. Stop going on at me. I'm sorry!" Lucia said angrily.

"So are the rest of us, unfortunately," sighed Uncle Lorenzo.

If only I could be like Giorgio, Tonino thought, as he got up from the table. I suppose what I should have to do is to find the words to the *Angel*. He went to school without seeing anything on the way, wondering how he could manage to do that, when the rest of his family had failed. He was realistic enough to know that he was simply not good enough at spells to make up the words in the ordinary way. It made him sigh heavily.

"Cheer up," said Paolo, as they went into school.

"I'm all right," Tonino said. He was surprised Paolo should think he was miserable. He was not miserable at all. He was wrapped in delightful dreams. Maybe I can do it by accident, he thought.

He sat in class composing strings of gibberish to the tune of the *Angel*, in hopes that some of it might be right. But that did not seem satisfactory, somehow. Then, in a lesson that was probably History – for he did not hear a word of it – it struck him, like a blinding light, what he had to do. He had to *find* the words, of course. The First Duke must have had them written down somewhere and lost the paper. Tonino was the boy whose mission it was to discover that lost paper. No nonsense about making up words, just straight detective work. And Tonino was positive that the book had been a clue. He must find a peeling blue house, and the paper with the words on would be somewhere near.

"Tonino," asked the teacher, for the fourth time, "where did Marco Polo journey to?"

Tonino did not hear the question, but he realised he was being asked something. "The Angel of Caprona," he said.

Nobody at school got much sense out of Tonino that day. He was full of the wonder of his discovery. It did not occur to him that Uncle Umberto had looked in every piece of writing in the University Library and not found the words to the *Angel*. Tonino knew.

After school, he avoided Paolo and his cousins. As soon as they were safely headed for the Casa Montana, Tonino set off in the opposite direction, towards the docks and quays by the New Bridge.

An hour later, Rosa said to Paolo, "What's the matter with Benvenuto? Look at him."

Paolo leant over the gallery rail beside her. Benvenuto, looking surprisingly small and piteous, was running backwards and forwards just inside the gate, mewing frantically. Every so often, as if he was too distracted to know what he was doing, he sat down, shot out a hind leg, and licked it madly. Then he leapt up and ran about again.

Paolo had never seen Benvenuto behave like this. He called out, "Benvenuto, what's the matter?"

Benvenuto swung round, crouching low on the ground, and stared urgently up at him. His eyes were like two yellow beacons of distress. He gave a string of mews, so penetrating and so demanding that Paolo felt his stomach turn uneasily.

"What *is* it, Benvenuto?" called Rosa.

Benvenuto's tail flapped in exasperation. He gave a great leap and vanished somewhere out of sight. Rosa and Paolo hung by their midriffs over the rail and craned after him. Benvenuto was now standing on the water butt, with his tail slashing. As soon as he knew they could see him, he stared fixedly at them again and uttered a truly appalling noise.

Wong wong wong wong-wong-wong!

Paolo and Rosa, without more ado, swung towards the stairs and clattered down them. Benvenuto's wails had already attracted all the other cats in the Casa. They were running across the yard and dropping from roofs before Paolo and Rosa were halfway down the stairs. They were forced to step carefully to the water butt among smooth furry bodies and staring, anxious green or yellow eyes.

"*Mee-ow-ow!*" Benvenuto said peremptorily, when they reached him.

He was thinner and browner than Paolo had ever seen him. There was a new rent in his left ear, and his coat was in ragged spikes. He looked truly wretched. "Mee-ow-ow!" he reiterated, from a wide pink mouth.

"Something's wrong," Paolo said uneasily. "He's trying to say something." Guiltily, he wished he had kept his resolution to learn to understand Benvenuto. But when Tonino could do it so easily, it had never been worth the bother. Now here was Benvenuto with an urgent message

– perhaps word from Chrestomanci – and he could not understand it. "We'd better get Tonino," he said.

Benvenuto's tail slashed again. "Mee-ow-ow!" he said, with tremendous force and meaning. Around Paolo and Rosa, the pink mouths of all the other cats opened too. "MEE-OW-OW!" It was deafening. Paolo stared helplessly.

It was Rosa who tumbled to their meaning. "Tonino!" she exclaimed. "They're saying *Tonino*! Paolo, where's Tonino?"

With a jolt of worry, Paolo realised he had not seen Tonino since breakfast. And as soon as he realised that, Rosa knew it too. And, such was the nature of the Casa Montana, that the alarm was given then and there. Aunt Gina shot out of the kitchen, holding a pair of kitchen tongs in one hand and a ladle in the other. Domenico and Aunt Maria came out of the Saloon, and Elizabeth appeared in the gallery outside the Music Room with the five little cousins. The door of the Scriptorium opened, filled with anxious faces.

Benvenuto gave a whisk of his tail and leapt for the gallery steps. He bounded up them, followed by the other cats; and Paolo and Rosa hurried up too, in a sort of shoal of leaping black and white bodies. Everyone converged on Antonio's rooms. People poured out of the Scriptorium, Elizabeth raced round the gallery, and Aunt Maria and Aunt Gina clambered up the steps by the kitchen quicker than either had ever climbed in her life. The Casa filled with the sound of hollow running feet.

The whole family jammed themselves after Rosa and

Paolo into the room where Tonino was usually to be found reading. There was no Tonino, only the red book lying on the windowsill. It was no longer shiny. The pages were thick at the edges and the red cover was curling upwards, as if the book was wet.

Benvenuto, with his jagged brown coat up in a ridge along his back and his tail fluffed like a fox's brush, landed on the sill beside the book and rashly put his nose forward to sniff at it. He leapt back again, shaking his head, crouching, and growling like a dog. Smoke poured up from the book. People coughed and cats sneezed. The book curled and writhed on the sill, amid clouds of smoke, exactly as if it were on fire. But instead of turning black, it turned pale grey-blue where it smoked, and looked slimy. The room filled with a smell of rotting.

"Ugh!" said everybody.

Old Niccolo barged members of his family right and left to get near it. He stood over it and sang, in a strong tenor voice almost as good as Marco's, three strange words. He sang them twice before he had to break off coughing. "Sing!" he croaked, with tears pouring down his face. "All of you."

All the Montanas obediently broke into song, three long notes in unison. And again. And again. After that, quite a number of them had to cough, though the smoke was distinctly less. Old Niccolo recovered and waved his arms, like the conductor of a choir. All who could, sang once more. It took ten repetitions to halt the decay of the book. By that time, it was a shrivelled triangle, about half the size it had been. Gingerly, Antonio leant over and opened the window beyond it, to let out the last of the smoke.

"What was it?" he asked Old Niccolo. "Someone trying to suffocate us all?"

"I thought it came from Umberto," Elizabeth faltered. "I never would have—"

Old Niccolo shook his head. "This thing never came from Umberto. And I don't think it was meant to kill. Let's see what kind of spell it is." He snapped his fingers and held out a hand, rather like a surgeon performing an operation. Without needing to be told, Aunt Gina put her kitchen tongs into his hand. Carefully, gently, Old Niccolo used the tongs to open the cover of the book.

"A good pair of tongs ruined," Aunt Gina said.

"Ssh!" said Old Niccolo. The shrivelled pages of the book had stuck into a gummy block. He snapped his fingers and held out his hand again. This time, Rinaldo put the pen he was carrying in it.

"And a good pen," he said, with a grimace at Aunt Gina.

With the pen as well as the tongs, Old Niccolo was able to pry the pages of the book apart without touching them and peel them over, one by one. Chins rested on both Paolo's shoulders as everyone craned to see, and there were chins on the shoulders of those with the chins. There was no sound but the sound of breathing.

On nearly every page, the printing had melted away, leaving a slimy, leathery surface quite unlike paper, with only a mark or so left in the middle. Old Niccolo looked closely at each mark and grunted. He grunted again at the first picture, which had faded like the print, but left a clearer mark. After that, though there was no print on any of the pages, the remaining mark was steadily clearer, up to the centre of the book, when it began to become more faded again, until the mark was barely visible on the back page.

Old Niccolo laid down the pen and the tongs in terrible silence. "Right through," he said at length. People shifted and someone coughed, but nobody said anything. "I do not know," said Old Niccolo, "the substance this object is made of, but I know a calling-charm when I see one. Tonino must have been like one hypnotised, if he had read all this."

"He *was* a bit strange at breakfast," Paolo whispered.

"I am sure he was," said his grandfather. He looked reflectively at the shrivelled stump of the book and then round at the crowded faces of his family. "Now who," he asked softly, "would want to set a strong calling-charm on Tonino Montana? Who would be mean enough to pick on a child? Who would—?" He turned suddenly on Benvenuto, crouched beside the book, and Benvenuto cowered right down, quivering, with his ragged ears flat against his flat head. "Where were you last night, Benvenuto?" he asked, more softly still.

No one understood the reply Benvenuto gave as he cowered, but everyone knew the answer. It was in Antonio and Elizabeth's harrowed faces, in the set of Rinaldo's chin, in Aunt Francesca's narrowed eyes, narrowed almost out of existence, and in the way Aunt Maria looked at Uncle Lorenzo; but most of all, it was in the way Benvenuto threw himself down on his side, with his back to the room, the picture of a cat in despair.

Old Niccolo looked up. "Now isn't that odd?" he said gently. "Benvenuto spent last night chasing a white she-cat – over the roofs of the Casa Petrocchi." He paused to let that sink in. "So Benvenuto," he said, "who knows a bad spell when he sees one, was not around to warn Tonino."

"But *why*?" Elizabeth asked despairingly.

Old Niccolo went, if possible, quieter still. "I can only conclude, my dear, that the Petrocchis are being paid by Florence, Siena, or Pisa."

There was another silence, thick and meaningful. Antonio broke it. "Well," he said, in such a subdued, grim way that Paolo stared at him. "Well? Are we going?"

"Of course," said Old Niccolo. "Domenico, fetch me my small black spell-book."

Everyone left the room, so suddenly, quietly and purposefully that Paolo was left behind, not clear what was going on. He turned uncertainly to go to the door, and realised that Rosa had been left behind too. She was sitting on Tonino's bed, with one hand to her head, white as Tonino's sheets.

"Paolo," she said, "tell Claudia I'll have the baby, if she wants to go. I'll have all the little ones."

She looked up at Paolo as she said it, and she looked so strange that Paolo was suddenly frightened. He ran gladly out into the gallery. The family was gathering, still quiet and grim, in the yard. Paolo ran down there and gave his message. Protesting little ones were pushed up the steps to Rosa, but Paolo did not help. He found Elizabeth and

Lucia and pushed close to them. Elizabeth put an arm round him and an arm round Lucia.

"Keep close to me, loves," she said. "I'll keep you safe." Paolo looked across her at Lucia and saw that Lucia was not frightened at all. She was excited. She winked at him. Paolo winked back and felt better.

A minute later, Old Niccolo took his place at the head of the family and they all hurried to the gate. Paolo had just forced his way through, jostling his mother on one side and Domenico on the other, when a carriage drew up in the road, and Uncle Umberto scrambled out of it. He came up to Old Niccolo in that grim, quiet way in which everyone seemed to be moving.

"Who is kidnapped? Bernardo? Domenico?"

"Tonino," replied Old Niccolo. "A book, with the University arms on the wrapping."

Uncle Umberto answered, "Luigi Petrocchi is also a member of the University."

"I bear that in mind," said Old Niccolo.

"I shall come with you to the Casa Petrocchi," said Uncle Umberto. He waved at the cab driver to tell him to go. The man was only too ready to. He nearly pulled his horses over on their sides, trying to turn them too quickly. The sight of the entire Casa Montana grimly streaming into the street seemed altogether too much for him.

That pleased Paolo. He looked back and forth as they swung down the Via Magica, and pride grew in him. There were such a lot of them. And they were so single-minded. The same intent look was in every face. And though children pattered and young men strode, though the ladies clattered on the cobbles in elegant shoes, though Old Niccolo's steps were short and bustling, and Antonio, because he could not wait to come at the Petrocchis, walked with long lunging steps, the common purpose gave the whole family a common rhythm. Paolo could almost believe they were marching in step.

The concourse crowded down the Via Sant' Angelo and swept round the corner into the Corso, with the Cathedral at their backs. People out shopping hastily gave them room. But Old Niccolo was too angry to use the pavement like a mere pedestrian. He led the family into the middle of the road and they marched there like a vengeful army, forcing cars and carriages to draw into the kerbs, with Old Niccolo stepping proudly at their head. It was hard to believe that a fat old man with a baby's face could look so warlike.

The Corso bends slightly beyond the Archbishop's Palace. Then it runs straight again by the shops, past the columns of the Art Gallery on one side and the gilded doors of the Arsenal on the other. They swung round that bend. There, approaching from the opposite direction, was another similar crowd, also walking in the road. The Petrocchis were on the march too.

"Extraordinary!" muttered Uncle Umberto.

"Perfect!" spat Old Niccolo.

The two families advanced on one another. There was utter silence now, except for the cloppering of feet. Every ordinary citizen, as soon as they saw the entire Casa Montana advancing on the entire Casa Petrocchi, made haste to get off the street. People knocked on the doors of perfect strangers and were let in without question. The manager of Grossi's, the biggest shop in Caprona, threw open his plate-glass doors and sent his assistants out to fetch in everyone nearby. After which he clapped the doors shut and locked a steel grille down in front of them. From between the bars, white faces stared out at the oncoming spell-makers. And a troop of Reservists, newly called up and sloppily marching in crumpled new uniforms, were horrified to find themselves caught between the two parties. They broke and ran, as one crumpled Reservist, and sought frantic shelter in the Arsenal. The great gilt doors clanged shut on them just as Old Niccolo halted, face to face with Guido Petrocchi.

"Well?" said Old Niccolo, his baby eyes glaring.

"Well?" retorted Guido, his red beard jutting.

"Was it," asked Old Niccolo, "Florence or Pisa that paid you to kidnap my grandson Tonino?"

Guido Petrocchi gave a bark of contemptuous laughter. "You mean," he said, "was it Pisa or Siena who paid *you* to kidnap my daughter Angelica?"

"Do you imagine," said Old Niccolo, "that saying that makes it any less obvious that you are a baby snatcher?"

"Do you," asked Guido, "accuse me of lying?"

"*Yes!*" roared the Casa Montana. "*Liar!*"

"*And the same to you!*" howled the Casa Petrocchi, crowding up behind Guido, lean and ferocious, many of them red-haired. "*Filthy liars!*"

The fighting began while they were still shouting. There was no knowing who started it. The roars on either side were mixed with singing and muttering. Scrips fluttered in many hands. And the air was suddenly full of flying eggs. Paolo received one, a very greasy fried egg, right across the mouth, and it made him so angry that he began to shout egg-spells too, at the top of his voice. Eggs splattered down, fried eggs, poached eggs, scrambled eggs, new-laid eggs, and eggs so horribly bad that they were like bombs when they burst. Everyone slithered on the eggy cobbles. Egg streamed off the ends of people's hair and spattered everyone's clothes.

Then somebody varied it with a bad tomato or so. Immediately, all manner of unpleasant things were flying about the Corso: cold spaghetti and cowpats – though these may have been Rinaldo's idea in the first place, they were very quickly coming from both sides – and cabbages; squirts of oil and showers of ice; dead rats and chicken livers.

It was no wonder that the ordinary people kept out of the way. Egg and tomato ran down the grilles over Grossi's windows and splashed the white columns of the Art Gallery. There were loud clangs as rotten cabbages hit the brass doors of the Arsenal.

This was the first, disorganised phase of the battle, with everyone venting his fury separately. But, by the time everyone was filthy and sticky, their fury took shape a little. Both sides began on a more organised chant. It grew, and became two strong rhythmic choruses.

The result was that the objects flying about the Corso rose up into the air and began to rain down as much more harmful things. Paolo looked up to see a cloud of transparent, glittering, frozen-looking pieces tumbling out of the sky at him. He thought it was snow at first, until a piece hit his arm and cut it.

"Vicious beasts!" Lucia screamed beside him. "It's broken glass!"

Before the main body of the glass came down, Old Niccolo's penetrating tenor voice soared above the yells and the chanting. "Testudo!"

Antonio's full bass backed him up: "Testudo!" and so did Uncle Lorenzo's baritone. Feet tramped. Paolo knew this one. He bowed over, tramping regularly, and kept up the charm with them. The whole family did it. *Tramp, tramp, tramp*. "Testudo, testudo, testudo!" Over their bent heads, the glass splinters bounced and showered harmlessly off an invisible barrier. "Testudo." From the middle of the bowed backs, Elizabeth's voice rang up sweetly in yet another spell. She was joined by Aunt Anna, Aunt Maria and Corinna. It was like a soprano descant over a rhythmic tramping chorus.

Paolo knew without being told that he must keep up the shield-charm while Elizabeth worked her spell. So did everyone else. It was extraordinary, exciting, amazing, he thought. Each Montana picked up the slightest hint and acted on it as if it were orders.

He risked glancing up and saw that the descant spell was working. Every glass splinter, as it hit the unseen shield Paolo was helping to make, turned into an angry hornet and buzzed back at the Petrocchis. But the Petrocchis simply turned them into glass splinters again and hurled them back. At the same time, Paolo could tell from the rhythm of their singing that some of them were working to destroy the shield-charm. Paolo sang and tramped harder than ever.

Meanwhile, Rinaldo's voice and his father's were singing gently, deeply, at work on something yet again. More of the ladies joined in the hornet-song so that the Petrocchis would not guess. And all the while, the tramp, tramp of the shield-charm was kept up by everyone else. It could have been the grandest chorus in the grandest opera ever, except that it all had a different purpose. The purpose came with a perfect roar of voices. The Petrocchis threw up their arms and staggered. The cobbles beneath them heaved and the solid Corso began to give way into a pit. Their instant reply was another huge sung chord, with discords innumerable. And the Montanas suddenly found themselves inside a wall of flame.

There was total confusion. Paolo staggered for safety, with his hair singed, over cobbles that quaked and heaved under his shoes. "Voltava!" he sang frantically. "Voltava!" Behind him, the flames hissed. Clouds of steam blotted out even the tall Art Gallery as the river answered the charm and came swirling up the Corso. Water was knee-deep round Paolo, up to his waist, and still rising. There was too much water. Someone had sung out of tune, and Paolo rather thought it was him. He saw his cousin Lena almost up to her chin in water and grabbed her. Towing Lena, he staggered through the current, over the heaving road, trying to make for the Arsenal steps.

Someone must have had the sense to work a cancel-spell. Everything suddenly cleared, steam, water and smoke together. Paolo found himself on the steps of the

Art Gallery, not by the Arsenal at all. Behind him, the Corso was a mass of loose cobbles, shiny with mud and littered with cowpats, tomatoes and fried eggs. There could hardly have been more mess if Caprona had been invaded by the armies of Florence, Pisa and Siena.

Paolo felt he had had enough. Lena was crying. She was too young. She should have been left with Rosa. He could see his mother picking Lucia out of the mud, and Rinaldo helping Aunt Gina up.

"Let's go home, Paolo," whimpered Lena.

But the battle was not really finished. Montanas and Petrocchis were up and down the Corso in little angry, muddy groups, shouting abuse at one another.

"I'll give you broken glass!"

"You started it!"

"You lying Petrocchi swine! Kidnapper!"

"Swine yourself! Spell-bungler! Traitor!"

Aunt Gina and Rinaldo slithered over to what looked like a muddy boulder in the street and heaved at it. The vast bulk of Aunt Francesca arose, covered with mud and angrier than Paolo had ever seen her.

"You filthy Petrocchis! I demand single combat!" she screamed. Her voice scraped like a great saw-blade and filled the Corso.

CHAPTER SEVEN

✳

*A*unt Francesca's challenge seemed to rally both sides. A female Petrocchi voice screamed, "We agree!" and all the muddy groups hastened towards the middle of the Corso again.

Paolo reached his family to hear Old Niccolo saying, "Don't be a fool, Francesca!" He looked more like a muddy goblin than the head of a famous family. He was almost too breathless to speak.

"They have insulted us and fought us!" said Aunt Francesca. "They deserve to be disgraced and drummed out of Caprona. And I shall do it! I'm more than a match for a Petrocchi!" She looked it, vast and muddy as she was, with her huge black dress in tatters and her grey hair half undone and streaming over one shoulder.

But the other Montanas knew Aunt Francesca was an old woman. There was a chorus of protest. Uncle Lorenzo and Rinaldo both offered to take on the Petrocchi champion in her place.

"No," said Old Niccolo. "Rinaldo, you were wounded—"

He was interrupted by catcalls from the Petrocchis. "Cowards! We want single combat!"

Old Niccolo's muddy face screwed up with anger. "Very well, they shall have their single combat," he said. "Antonio, I appoint you. Step forward."

Paolo felt a gush of pride. So his father was, as he had always thought, the best spell-maker in the Casa Montana. But the pride became mixed with alarm, when Paolo saw the way his mother clutched Antonio's arm, and the worried, reluctant look on his father's mud-streaked face.

"Go on!" Old Niccolo said crossly.

Slowly, Antonio advanced into the space between the two families, stumbling a little among the loose cobbles. "I'm ready," he called to the Petrocchis. "Who's your champion?"

It was clear that there was some indecision among the Petrocchis. A dismayed voice said, "It's *Antonio*!" This was followed by a babble of talk. From the turning of heads and the uncertain heaving about, Paolo thought they were looking for a Petrocchi who was unaccountably missing. But the fuss died away, and Guido Petrocchi himself stepped forward. Paolo could see several Petrocchis looking as alarmed as Elizabeth.

"I'm ready too," said Guido, baring his teeth angrily.

Since his face was plastered with mud, it made him look quite savage. He was also large and sturdy. He made Antonio look small, gentle and fragile. "And I demand an unlimited contest!" snarled Guido. He seemed even angrier than Old Niccolo.

"Very well," Antonio said. There could have been the least shake in his voice. "You're aware that means a fight to the finish, are you?"

"Suits me perfectly," said Guido. He was like a giant saying "Fee-fi-fo-fum". Paolo was suddenly very frightened.

It was at this moment that the Ducal Police arrived. They had come in, quietly and cunningly, riding bicycles along the pavements. No one noticed them until the Chief of Police and his lieutenant were standing beside the two champions.

"Guido Petrocchi and Antonio Montana," said the lieutenant, "I arrest you—"

Both champions jumped, and turned to find blue braided uniforms on either side of them.

"Oh go away," said Old Niccolo, hastening forward. "What do you have to interfere for?"

"Yes, go away," said Guido. "We're busy."

The lieutenant flinched at Guido's face, but the Chief of Police was a bold and dashing man with a handsome moustache, and he had his reputation to keep up as a bold and dashing man. He bowed to Old Niccolo. "These two are under arrest," he said. "The rest of you I order to sink your differences and remember there is about to be a war."

"We're at war already," said Old Niccolo. "Go away."

"I regret," said the Chief of Police, "that that is impossible."

"Then don't say you weren't warned," said Guido.

There was a short burst of song from the adults of both families. Paolo wished he knew that spell. It sounded useful. As soon as it was over, Rinaldo and a swarthy young Petrocchi came over to the two policemen and towed them away backwards. They were as stiff as the tailor's dummies in the barred windows of Grossi's. Rinaldo and the other young man laid them against the steps of the Art Gallery and returned each to his family, without looking at one another. As for the rest of the Ducal Police, they seemed to have vanished, bicycles and all.

"Ready now?" said Guido.

"Ready," said Antonio.

And the single combat commenced.

Looking back on it afterwards, Paolo realised that it could not have lasted more than three minutes, though it seemed endless at the time. For, in that time, the strength, skill and speed of both champions was tried to the utmost. The first, and probably the longest, part was when the two were testing one another for an opening, and comparatively little seemed to happen. Both stood, leaning slightly forward, muttering, humming, occasionally flicking a hand.

Paolo stared at his father's strained face and wondered just what was going on. Then, momentarily, Guido was a man-shaped red-and-white check duster. Someone gasped. But Antonio almost simultaneously became a cardboard man covered with green triangles. Then both flicked back to themselves again.

The speed of it astounded Paolo. A spell had not only been cast on both sides, but also a counter-spell, and a spell counter to that, all in the time it took someone to gasp. Both combatants were panting and looking warily at each other. It was clear they were very evenly matched.

Again there was a space when nothing seemed to happen, except a sort of flickering on both sides. Then suddenly Antonio struck, and struck so hard that it was plain he had all the time been building a strong spell, beneath the flicker of trivial spells designed to keep Guido occupied. Guido gave a shout and dissolved into dust, which swept away backwards in a spiral. But, somehow, as he dissolved, he threw *his* strong spell at Antonio. Antonio broke into a thousand little pieces, like a spilt jigsaw puzzle.

For an ageless time, the swirl of dust and the pile of broken Antonio hung in mid-air. Both were struggling to stay together and not to patter down on the uprooted cobbles of the Corso. In fact, they were still struggling to make spells too. When, at last, Antonio staggered forward in one piece, holding some kind of red fruit in his right hand, he had barely time to dodge. Guido was a leopard in mid-spring.

Elizabeth screamed.

Antonio threw himself to one side, heaved a breath and sang. "*Oliphans!*" His usually silky voice was rough and ragged, but he hit the right notes. A gigantic elephant, with tusks longer than Paolo was tall, cut off the low sun and shook the Corso as it advanced, ears spread, to trample the attacking leopard. It was hard to believe the great beast was indeed worried, thin Antonio Montana.

For a shadow of a second, the leopard was Guido Petrocchi, very white in the face and luridly red in the beard, gabbling a frantic song. *"Hickory-dickory-muggery-mus!"* And he must have hit the right notes too. He seemed to vanish.

The Montanas were raising a cheer at Guido's cowardice, when the elephant panicked. Paolo had the merest glimpse of a little tiny mouse scampering aggressively at the great front feet of the elephant, before he was running for his life. The shrill trumpeting of Antonio seemed to tear his ears apart. Behind him, Paolo knew that the elephant was stark, staring mad, trampling this way and that among terrified Montanas. Lucia ran past him, carrying Lena clutched backwards against her front. Paolo grabbed little Bernardo by one arm and ran with him, wincing at the horrible brazen, braying squeal from his father.

Elephants are afraid of mice, horribly afraid. And there are very few people who can shift shape without taking the nature of the shape they shift to. It seemed that Guido Petrocchi had not only won, but got most of the Montanas trampled to death into the bargain.

But when Paolo next looked, Elizabeth was standing in the elephant's path, staring up at its wild little eyes. "Antonio!" she shouted. *"Antonio*, control yourself!" She looked so tiny and the elephant was coming so fast that Paolo shut his eyes.

He opened them in time to see the elephant in the act of swinging his mother up on its back. Tears of relief so clouded Paolo's eyes that he almost failed to see Guido's next attack. He was simply aware of a shattering noise, a horrible smell, and a sort of moving tower. He saw the elephant swing round, and Elizabeth crouch down on its back. It was now being confronted by a vast iron machine, even larger than itself, throbbing with mechanical power and filling the Corso with nasty blue smoke. This thing ground slowly towards Antonio on huge moving tracks. As it came, a gun in its front swung down to aim between the elephant's eyes.

On the spur of the moment, Antonio became another machine. He was in such a hurry, and he knew so little about machines, that it was a very bizarre machine indeed. It was pale duck-egg blue, with enormous rubber wheels. In fact, it was probably made of rubber all through, because the bullet from Guido's machine bounced off it and crashed into the steps of the Arsenal. Most people threw themselves flat.

"Mother's *inside* that thing!" Lucia screamed to Paolo, above the noise.

Paolo realised she must be. Antonio had had no time to put Elizabeth down. And now he was barging recklessly at Guido, *bang*-bounce, *bang*-bounce. It must have been horrible for Elizabeth. Luckily, it only lasted a second. Elizabeth and Antonio suddenly appeared in their own shapes, almost under the mighty tracks of the Guido-machine. Elizabeth ran – Paolo had not known she could run so fast – like the wind towards the Arsenal. And it may have been Petrocchi viciousness, or perhaps simple confusion, but the great Guido-tank swung its gun down to point at Elizabeth.

Antonio called Guido a very bad name, and threw the tomato he still had in his hand. The red fruit hit, and splashed, and ran down the iron side. Paolo was just wondering what use that was, when the tank was not there any more. Nor was Guido. In his place was a giant tomato. It was about the size of a pumpkin. And it simply sat in the road and did not move.

That was the winning stroke. Paolo could tell it was from the look on Antonio's face as he walked up to the tomato. Disgusted and weary, Antonio bent down to pick up the tomato. There were scattered groans from the Petrocchis, and cheers, not quite certain and even more scattered, from the Montanas.

Then somebody cast yet another spell.

This time, it was a thick wet fog. No doubt, at the beginning, it would not have seemed so terrible, but, after all the rest, just when the fight was over, Paolo felt it was the last straw. All he could see, in front of his eyes, was thick whiteness. After he had taken a breath or so, he was coughing.

He could hear coughing all round, and far off into the distance, which was the only thing which showed him he was not entirely alone. He turned his head from trying to see who else was coughing, and found he could not see Lucia. Nor could he find Bernardo, and he knew he had been holding Bernardo's arm a second before. As soon as he realised that, he found he had lost his sense of direction too. He was all alone, coughing and shivering, in cold white emptiness.

"I am *not* going to lose my head," Paolo told himself sternly. "My father didn't, and so I shan't. I shall find somewhere to shelter until this beastly spell is over. Then I shall go home. I don't care if Tonino *is* still missing—" He stopped then, because a thought came to him, like an astonishing discovery. "We're never going to find Tonino this way, anyway," he said. And he knew it was true.

With his hands stretched out in front of him and his eyes spread very wide in hopes of seeing something – which was unlikely, since they were streaming from the fog, and so was his nose – Paolo coughed and sniffed and shuffled his way forward until his toes came up against stone. Paolo looked down, but he could not see what it was. He tried lifting one foot, with his toes scraping against the obstruction. And, after a few inches, the obstruction stopped and his foot shot forward. It was a ledge, then. Probably the kerb. He had been near the edge of the road when he ran away from the elephant. He got both feet on the kerb and shuffled forward six inches – then he fell upstairs over what seemed to be a body.

It gave Paolo such a shock that he dared not move at first. But he soon realised the body beneath him was shivering, as he was, and trying to cough and mutter at the same time. "Holy Mary—" Paolo heard, in a hoarse blurred voice. Very puzzled, Paolo put out a careful hand and felt the body. His fingers met cold metal buttons, uniform braid, and, a little above that, a warm face – which gave a croak as Paolo's cold hand met its mouth – and a large furry moustache beneath the nose.

Angel of Caprona! Paolo thought. It's the Chief of Police!

Paolo got himself to his knees on what must be the steps of the Art Gallery. There was no one around he could ask, but it did not seem fair to leave someone lying helpless in the fog. It was bad enough if you could move. So hoping he was doing the right thing, Paolo knelt and sang, very softly, the most general cancel-spell he could think of. It had no effect on the fog – that was evidently very strong magic – but he heard the Chief of Police roll over on his side and groan. Boots scraped as he tested his legs. "*Mamma mia!*" Paolo heard him moan.

He sounded as if he wanted to be alone. Paolo left him and crawled his way up the Gallery steps. He had no idea he had reached the top, until he hit his elbow on a pillar and drove his head into Lucia's stomach at the same moment. Both of them said some extremely unpleasant things.

"When you've quite finished swearing," Lucia said at length, "you can get between these pillars with me and keep me warm." She coughed and shivered. "Isn't this awful? Who did it?" She coughed again. The fog had made her hoarse.

"It wasn't us," said Paolo. "We'd have known. Ow, my elbow!" He took hold of her for a guide and wedged himself down beside her. He felt better like that.

"The pigs," said Lucia. "I call this a mean trick. It's funny – you spend your life being told what pigs they are, and thinking they *can't* be, really. Then you meet them, and they're worse than you were told. Was it you singing just now?"

"I fell over the Chief of Police on the steps," said Paolo.

Lucia laughed. "I fell over the other one. I sang a cancel-spell too. He was lying on all the corners of the stairs and it must have bruised him all over when I fell on him."

"It's bad enough when you can move," Paolo agreed. "Like being blind."

"Horrible," said Lucia. "That blind beggar in the Via Sant' Angelo – I shall give him some money tomorrow."

"The one with white eyes?" said Paolo. "Yes, so shall I. And I never want to see another spell."

"To tell you the truth," said Lucia, "I was wishing I dared burn the Library and the Scriptorium down. It came to me like a blinding flash – just before I fell over that policeman – that no amount of spells are going to work on those beastly kidnappers."

"That's just what I thought!" exclaimed Paolo. "I know the only way to find Tonino—"

"Hang on," said Lucia. "I think the fog's getting thinner."

She was right. When Paolo leant forward, he could see two dark lumps below, where the Chief of Police and his lieutenant were sitting on the steps with their heads in their hands. He could see quite a stretch of the Corso beyond them – cobbles which were dark and wet-looking, but, to his surprise, neither muddy nor out of place.

"Someone's put it all back!" said Lucia.

The fog thinned further. They could see the glimmering

doors of the Arsenal now, and the entire foggy width of the Corso, with every cobblestone back where it should be. Somewhere about the middle of it, Antonio and Guido Petrocchi were standing facing one another.

"Oh, they're not going to begin again, are they?" wailed Paolo.

But, almost at once, Antonio and Guido swung round and walked away from one another.

"Thank goodness!" said Lucia. She and Paolo turned to one another, smiling with relief.

Except that it was not Lucia. Paolo found himself staring into a white pointed face, and eyes darker, larger and shrewder than Lucia's. Surrounding the face were draggled dark red curls. The smile died from the face and horror replaced it as Paolo stared. He felt his own face behaving the same way. He had been huddling up against a Petrocchi! He knew which one, too. It was the elder of the two who had been at the palace. Renata, that was her name. And she knew him too.

"You're that blue-eyed Montana boy!" she exclaimed. She made it sound quite disgusting.

Both of them got up. Renata backed into the pillars, as if she was trying to get inside the stone, and Paolo backed away along the steps.

"I thought you were my sister Lucia," he said.

"I thought you were my cousin Claudio," Renata retorted.

Somehow, they both made it sound as if it was the other one's fault.

"It wasn't my fault!" Paolo said angrily. "Blame the

person who made the fog, not me. There's an enemy enchanter."

"I know. Chrestomanci said," said Renata.

Paolo felt he hated Chrestomanci. He had no business to go and say the same things to the Petrocchis as he said to the Montanas. But he hated the enemy enchanter even more. He had been responsible for the most embarrassing thing which had ever happened to Paolo. Muttering with shame, Paolo turned to run away.

"No, stop! *Wait!*" Renata said. She said it so commandingly that Paolo stopped without thinking, and gave Renata time to snatch hold of his arm. Instead of pulling away, Paolo stood quite still and attempted to behave with the dignity becoming to a Montana. He looked at his arm, and at Renata's hand holding it, as if both had become one composite slimy toad. But Renata hung on. "Look all you like," she said. "I don't care. I'm not letting go until you tell me what your family has done with Angelica."

"Nothing," Paolo said contemptuously. "We wouldn't touch one of you with a barge-pole. What have you lot done with Tonino?"

An odd little frown wrinkled Renata's white forehead. "Is that your brother? Is he really missing?"

"He was sent a book with a calling-spell in it," said Paolo.

"A book," said Renata slowly, "got Angelica too. We only realised when it shrivelled away."

She let go of Paolo's arm. They stared at one another in the blowing remains of the fog.

"It must be the enemy enchanter," said Paolo.

"Trying to take our minds off the war," said Renata. "Tell your family, won't you?"

"If you tell yours," said Paolo.

"Of course I will. What do you take me for?" said Renata.

In spite of everything, Paolo found himself laughing. "I think you're a Petrocchi!" he said.

But when Renata began to laugh too, Paolo realised it was too much. He turned to run away, and found himself facing the Chief of Police. The Chief of Police had evidently recovered his dignity. "Now then, you children. Move along," he said.

Renata fled, without more ado, red in the face with the shame of being caught talking to a Montana. Paolo hung on. It seemed to him that he ought to report that Tonino was missing.

"I said move along!" repeated the Chief of Police, and he pulled down his jacket with a most threatening jerk.

Paolo's nerve broke. After all, an ordinary policeman was not going to be much help against an enchanter. He ran.

He ran all the way to the Casa Montana. The fog and the wetness did not extend beyond the Corso. As soon as he turned into a side road, Paolo found himself in the bleak shadows and low red sun of a winter evening. It was like being shot back into another world – a world where things happened as they should, where one's father did not turn into a mad elephant, where, above all, one's sister did not turn out to be a Petrocchi.

Paolo's face fired with shame as he ran. Of all the awful things to happen!

The Casa Montana came in sight, with the familiar Angel safely over the gate. Paolo shot in under it, and ran into his father. Antonio was standing under the archway, panting as if he too had run all the way home.

"Who!? Oh, Paolo," said Antonio. "Stay where you are."

"Why?" asked Paolo. He wanted to get in, where it was safe, and perhaps eat a large lump of bread and honey. He was surprised his father did not feel the same. Antonio looked tired out, and his clothes were torn and muddy rags. The arm he stretched out to keep Paolo in the gateway was half bare and covered with scratches. Paolo was going to protest, when he saw that something was indeed wrong. Most of the cats were in the gateway too, crouching around with their ears flattened. Benvenuto was patrolling the entrance to the yard, like a lean brown ferret. Paolo could hear him growling.

Antonio's scratched hand took Paolo by the shoulder and pulled him forward so that he could see into the yard. "Look."

Paolo found himself blinking at foot-high letters, which seemed to hang in the air in the middle of the yard. In the fading light, they were glowing an unpleasant, sick yellow.

STOP ALL SPELLS OR YOUR CHILD SUFFERS.
CASA PETROCCHI

The name was in sicker and brighter letters. They were meant to make no mistake about who had sent the message.

After what Renata had said, Paolo knew it was wrong. "It *wasn't* the Petrocchis," he said. "It's that enchanter Chrestomanci told us about."

"Yes, to be sure," said Antonio.

Paolo looked up at him and saw that his father did not believe him – probably had not even attended to him. "But it's true!" he said. "He wants us to stop making war-spells."

Antonio sighed, and drew himself together to explain to Paolo. "Paolo," he said, "nobody but Chrestomanci believes in this enchanter. In magic, as in everything else, the simplest explanation is always best. In other words, why invent an unknown enchanter, when you have a known enemy with known reasons for hating you? Why shouldn't it be the Petrocchis?"

Paolo wanted to protest, but he was still too embarrassed about Renata to say that Angelica Petrocchi was missing too. He was struggling to find something that he *could* say, which might convince his father, when a square of light sprang up in the gallery as a door there opened.

"Rosa!" shouted Antonio. His voice cracked with anxiety.

The shape of Rosa appeared in the light, carrying Cousin Claudia's baby. The light itself was so orange and so bright, beside the sick glow of the letters floating in the yard, that Paolo was flooded with relief.

Behind Rosa, there was Marco, carrying another little one.

"Praised be!" said Antonio. He shouted, "Are you all right, Rosa? How did those words come here?"

"We don't know," Rosa called back. "They just appeared. We've been trying to get rid of them, but we can't."

Marco leant over the rails and called, "It's not true, Antonio. The Petrocchis wouldn't do a thing like this."

Antonio called back, "Don't go around saying that, Marco." He said it so forbiddingly that Paolo knew nothing he said was going to be believed. If he had had a chance of convincing Antonio, he had now lost it.

CHAPTER EIGHT

✸

When Tonino came to his senses – at, incidentally, the precise moment when the enchanted book began to shrivel away – he had, at first, a nightmare feeling that he was shut in a cardboard box. He rolled his head sideways on his arms. He seemed to be lying on his face on a hard but faintly furry floor. In the far distance, he could blurrily see someone else, leaning up against a wall like a doll, but he felt too queer to be very interested in that. He rolled his head round the other way and saw the panels of a wall quite near. That told him he was in a fairly long room. He rolled his head to stare down at the furry floor. It was patterned, in a pattern too big for his eyes to grasp, and he supposed it was a carpet of some kind. He shut his blurry eyes and tried to think what had happened.

He remembered going down near the New Bridge. He had been full of excitement. He had read a book which he thought was telling him how to save Caprona. He knew he had to find an alleyway with a peeling blue house at the end of it. It seemed a bit silly now. Tonino knew things never happened the way they did in books. Even then, he had been rather amazed to find that there *was* an alleyway with, really and truly, a peeling blue house at the end of it. And, to his huge excitement, there was a scrap of paper fluttering down at his feet. The book was coming true. Tonino had bent down and picked up the paper.

And, after that, he had known nothing till this moment.

That was really true. Tonino took himself through what had happened several times, but each time his memories stopped in exactly the same place – with himself picking up the scrap of paper. After that, it was all a vague sense of nightmare. By this time, he was fairly sure he had been the victim of a spell. He began to feel ashamed of himself. So he sat up.

He saw at once why he had seemed to dream he was shut up in a cardboard box. The room he was in was long and low, almost exactly the shape of a shoebox. The walls and ceiling were painted cream-colour – a sort of whitish cardboard-colour, in fact – but they seemed to be wood, because there were carvings picked out in gold paint on them. There was a crystal chandelier hanging from the ceiling, although the light came from four long windows in one of the longer walls; a rich carpet on the floor, and a very elegant dining-table and chairs by the wall opposite the windows. There were two silver candlesticks on the table. Altogether the place was extremely elegant – and wrong, somehow.

Tonino sat trying to puzzle out just what was wrong. The room was awfully bare. But that was not quite it. There was something strange about the daylight coming through the four long windows, as if the sun was somehow further away than it should be. But that was not quite it either. Tonino's eyes went to the four bands of too-faded sunlight falling through the windows on to the carpet, and then travelled along the carpet. At the end, he came to the person leaning up against the wall. It was Angelica Petrocchi, who had been at the Palace. Her eyes were closed beneath her bulge of forehead, and she looked ill. So she had been caught too.

Tonino looked back at the carpet. That was an odd thing. It was not really a carpet. It had been painted on the slightly furry substance of the floor. Tonino could see the brush-strokes in the sprawling pattern. And the reason he had thought the pattern was too big, was because it *was* too big. It was the wrong size for the rest of the room.

More puzzled than ever, Tonino struggled to his feet. He felt a little wobbly, so he put a hand on the gilded panels of the wall to steady himself. That felt furry too, except where it was gold. The gold was flat, but not quite hard, like – Tonino thought, but no other likeness came to him – like paint. He ran his hand over the apparently carved panel. It was a total cheat. It was not even wood, and the carving was painted on, in lines of brown, blue and gold. Whoever had caught him was trying to seem richer than they were, but doing it very badly.

There were movements at the other end of the room. Angelica Petrocchi was wavering to her feet, and she too was running her hand over the painted carving. Very anxiously and cautiously, she turned and looked at Tonino.

"Will you let me go now, please?" she said.

There was a little wobble in her voice that showed Tonino she was very frightened. So was he, now he came to think of it. "I can't let you go," he said. "I didn't catch you. Neither of us can go. There isn't a door."

That was the wrong thing he had been trying not to notice. And as soon as he said it, he wished he had kept his mouth shut. Angelica screamed. And the sound sent Tonino into a panic too. There was no door! He was shut into a cardboard box with a Petrocchi child!

Tonino may have screamed as well – he was not sure. When he caught up with himself, he had one of the elegant chairs in his hands and was battering at the nearest window with it. That was more frightening than ever. The glass did not break. It was made of some slightly rubbery stuff, and the chair bounced off. Beyond him, the Petrocchi girl was banging away at another window with one of the silver candlesticks, screaming all the time. Outside the window, Tonino could clearly see the smug spire-shape of a little cypress tree, lit by afternoon sun. So they were in one of those rich villas near the Palace, were they? Just let him get *out*! He lifted the chair and smashed it against the window with all his strength.

He made no impression on the window, but the chair came to pieces. Two ill-glued legs fell off it, and the rest crumpled to splintery matchwood. Tonino thought it was disgustingly badly made. He threw it to the painted carpet and fetched another chair. This time, for variety, he attacked the wall beside the window. Pieces of that chair came away and flew about, and Tonino was left with its painted seat – painted to look like embroidery, just as the floor was painted to look like carpet. He drove it into the wall, again and again. It made large brown dents. Better still, the wall shook and leapt about, sounding muffled and hollow, as if it were made of something very cheap. Tonino beat at it and yelled. Angelica beat at the wall and the window impartially with her candlestick, and went on screaming.

They were stopped by a terrible hammering. Someone seemed to be dealing hundreds of thunderous blows on the ceiling. The room was like the inside of a drum. It was too loud to bear. The Petrocchi girl dropped her candlestick and rolled on the floor. Tonino found himself crouching down, with his hands to his ears, looking up at the chandelier jiggling overhead. He thought his head would burst.

The pounding stopped. There was no sound except a whimper, which Tonino rather thought came from him.

A great huge voice spoke through the ceiling. "That's better. Now be quiet, or you won't get any food. And if you try any more tricks, you'll be punished. Understand?"

Tonino and Angelica both sat up. "*Let us out!*" they screamed.

There was no answer, only a distant shuffling. The owner of the huge voice seemed to be going away.

"A mean trick with an amplifying spell," Angelica said.

She picked up the candlestick and looked at it with disgust. The branched part was bent at right-angles to the base. "What *is* this place?" she said. "Everything's so shoddy."

They got up and went to the windows again, in hopes of a clue. Several little spire-shaped trees were clearly to be seen, just outside, and a sort of terrace beyond that. But, peer as they might, all they could make out further off was queer blue distance, with one or two square-shaped mountains catching the sun on a glossy corner or so. There seemed to be no sky.

"It's a spell," said Angelica. Her voice suggested she might be going to panic again. "A spell to stop us knowing where we are."

Tonino supposed it must be. There was no other way of accounting for the strange absence of view. "But I'm sure I know," he said, "by those trees. We're in one of those rich villas by the Palace."

"You're right," agreed Angelica. The panic had left her voice. "I shall never envy those people again. Their lives are all show."

They turned from the windows and discovered that the vast banging had dislodged one of the wall panels behind the dining-table. It hung open like a door. They shoved one another out of the way to reach it first. But there was only a cupboard-sized bathroom, without a window.

"Good," said Angelica. "I was wondering what we'd do. And at least we'll have water." She reached out to one of the taps over the small washbasin. It came away in her hand. Under it was a blob of glue on white china. It was clear the tap had never been meant to be used. Angelica stared at it with such a ridiculous look of bewilderment that Tonino laughed. She drew herself up at that. "Don't you laugh at me, you beastly Montana!" She stalked out into the main room and threw the useless tap on to the table with a clump. Then she sat in one of the two remaining chairs and rested her elbows gloomily on the table.

After a while, Tonino did the same. The chair creaked under him. So did the table. Though its surface was painted to look like smooth mahogany, close to, it was all blobs of varnish and huge splinters. "There's nothing that's not shoddy," he said.

"Including you, Whatyoumecall Montana!" Angelica said. She was still angry.

"My name's Tonino," Tonino said.

"It's the last twist of the knife, being shut up with a Montana!" Angelica said. "Whatever your name is. I shall have to put up with all your filthy habits."

"Well, I've got to put up with yours," Tonino said irritably. It suddenly struck him that he was all alone, far from the friendly bustle of the Casa Montana. Even when he was hidden in a corner of the Casa with a book, he knew the rest of the family was all round him. And Benvenuto would be purring and pricking him, to remind him he was not alone. Dear old Benvenuto. Tonino was afraid he was going to cry – in front of a Petrocchi too. "How did they catch you?" he said, to take his mind off it.

"With a book." A slight, woeful smile appeared on Angelica's tight white face. "It was called *The Girl Who*

Saved Her Country, and I thought it was from Great-Uncle Luigi. I still think it was a good story." She looked defiantly at Tonino.

Tonino was annoyed. It was not pleasant to think he had been caught by the same spell as a Petrocchi. "Me too," he said gruffly.

"And *I* haven't got any filthy habits!" snapped Angelica.

"Yes you have. All the Petrocchis have," said Tonino. "But I expect you don't realise because they're normal to you."

"I like that!" Angelica picked up the broken tap, as if she had half a mind to throw it.

"I don't care about your habits," said Tonino. Nor did he. All he wanted to do was find some way out of this nightmare room and go home. "How shall we get out of here?"

"Through the ceiling," Angelica said sarcastically.

Tonino looked upwards. There was that chandelier. If they could give it a pull, it might well rip a hole in the shoddy ceiling.

"Don't be stupid," said Angelica. "If there's a spell out in front, there's bound to be one up there to stop us getting out."

Tonino feared she was right, but it was worth a try. He climbed from his chair on to the table. He thought he could reach the chandelier from there if he stood up. There was a violent creaking. Before Tonino could begin to stand up, the table swayed away sideways, as if all four of its legs were loose.

"Get down!" said Angelica.

Tonino got down. It was clear the table would fall to pieces if he stayed on it. Gloomily he pushed the crooked legs straight again. "So that's no good," he said.

"Unless," said Angelica, suddenly bright and pert, "we steady it with a spell."

Tonino transferred his miserable look from the table legs to her sharp little face. He sighed. The subject had been bound to come up. "You'll have to do the spell," he said. Angelica stared at him. He could feel his face heating up. "I hardly know any spells," he said. "I – I'm slow."

He had expected Angelica to laugh, and she did. But he thought she need not have laughed in such a mean, exultant way, nor keep saying, "Oh that's good!" like that.

"What's so funny?" he said. "You can laugh! I know all about you turning your father green. You're no better than me!"

"Want to bet?" said Angelica, still laughing.

"No," said Tonino. "Just make the spell."

"I can't," said Angelica. It was Tonino's turn to stare, and Angelica's turn to blush. A thin bright pink spread right up the bulge of her forehead, and she put her chin up defiantly. "I'm hopeless at spells," she said. "I've never got a spell right in my life." Seeing Tonino still staring, she said, "It's a pity you didn't bet. I'm *much* worse than you are."

Tonino could not credit it. "How?" he said. "Why? Can't you learn spells either, then?"

"Oh, I can *learn* them all right." Angelica took up the broken tap again and scribbled angrily with it, great yellow scratches in the varnished top of the table. "I know hundreds of spells," she said, "but I always get them wrong. For a start, I'm tone-deaf. I can't sing a tune right to save my life. Like now." Carefully, as if she was a craftsman doing a fine carving, she peeled up a long yellow curl of varnish from the table, using the tap as a gouge. "But it's not only that," she said angrily, following her work intently. "I get words wrong too – everything wrong. And my spells always work, that's the worst of it. I've turned all my family all colours of the rainbow. I've turned the baby's bath into wine, and the wine into gravy. I turned my own head back to front once. I'm much worse than you. I *daren't* do spells. About all I'm good for is understanding cats. And I even turned my cat purple too."

Tonino watched her working away with the tap, with rather mixed feelings. If you looked at it practically, this was the worst possible news. Neither of them had a hope against the powerful spell-maker who had caught them. On the other hand, he had never met anyone who was worse at spells than he was. He thought, a little smugly, that at least he had never made a mistake in a spell, and that made him feel good. He wondered how the Casa Montana would feel if he kept turning them all colours of the rainbow. He imagined the stern Petrocchis must hate it. "Doesn't your family mind?" he asked.

"Not much," Angelica said, surprisingly. "They don't mind it half as much as I do. Everyone has a good laugh every time I make a new mistake – but they don't let anyone talk about it outside the Casa. Papa says I'm notorious enough for turning him green, and he doesn't like me to be even *seen* anywhere until I've grown out of it."

"But you went to the Palace," said Tonino. He thought Angelica must be exaggerating.

"Only because Cousin Monica was having her baby and everyone was so busy on the Old Bridge," said Angelica. "He had to take Renata off her shift and get my brother out of bed to drive the coach, in order to have enough of us."

"There were five of us," Tonino said, smugly.

"Our horses collapsed in the rain." Angelica turned from her gouging and looked at Tonino keenly. "So my brother said yours were bound to have collapsed too, because *you* only had a cardboard coachman."

Uncomfortably, Tonino knew Angelica had scored a point. "Our coachman collapsed too," he admitted.

"I thought so," said Angelica, "from the look on your face." She went back to scraping the table, conscious of victory.

"It wasn't our fault!" Tonino protested. "Chrestomanci says there's an enemy enchanter."

Angelica took such a slice out of the varnish that the table swooped sideways and Tonino had to push it straight. "And he's got us now," she said. "And he's taken care to get the two who are no good at spells. So how do we get out of here and spite him, Tonino Montana? Any ideas?"

Tonino sat with his chin in his hands and thought. He had read enough books, for goodness sake. People were always being kidnapped in books. And in his favourite books – this was like a bad joke – they escaped without using magic of any kind. But there was no door. That was what made it seem impossible. Wait a moment! The vast voice had promised them food. "If they think we're behaving," he said, "they'll bring us supper probably. And they've got to bring the food in somehow. If we watch where it comes in, we ought to be able to get out the same way."

"There's bound to be a spell on the entrance," Angelica said gloomily.

"Do stop bleating away about spells," said Tonino. "Don't you Petrocchis ever talk about anything else?"

Angelica did not reply, but simply scraped away with her tap. Tonino sat wanly in his creaking chair thinking over the few spells he really knew. The most useful seemed to be a simple cancel-spell.

"A cancel-spell," Angelica said irritatingly, scratching carefully with the tap. The floor round her feet was heaped with yellow curls of varnish. "That might hold the entrance open. Or isn't a cancel-spell one of the ones you know?"

"I know a cancel-spell," said Tonino.

"So does my baby brother," said Angelica. "He'd probably be more use."

Their supper arrived. It appeared, without warning, on a tray, floating towards them from the windows. It took Tonino completely by surprise.

"*Spell!*" Angelica squawked at him. "Don't just stare!"

Tonino sang the spell. Hurried and surprised though he was, he was *sure* he got it right. But it was the tray the spell worked on. The tray, and the food on it, began to grow. Within seconds, it was bigger than the table-top. And it still floated towards the table, growing as it came. Tonino found himself backing away from two steaming bath-sized bowls of soup and two great orange thickets of spaghetti, all of which were getting steadily vaster the nearer they came. By now, there was not much room round the edges of the tray. Tonino backed against the end wall, wondering if Angelica's trouble with spells was catching. Angelica herself was squashed against the bathroom door. Both of them were in danger of being cut in two.

"Get down on the floor!" Tonino shouted.

They slithered hurriedly down the wall, underneath the tray, which hung over them like a too-low ceiling. The huge odour of spaghetti was quite oppressive.

"What have you done?" Angelica said, coming towards Tonino on hands and knees. "You didn't get it right."

"Yes, but if it gets much bigger, it might break the room open," said Tonino.

Angelica sank back on her knees and looked at him with what was nearly respect. "That's almost a good idea."

But it was only almost. The tray certainly met all four walls. They heard it thump against them. There was a deal of swaying, creaking and squeezing, from the tray and from the walls, but the walls did not give. After a moment it was clear that the tray was not being allowed to get any bigger.

"There *is* a spell on this room," Angelica said. It was not meant to be I-told-you-so. She was miserable.

Tonino gave up and sang the cancel-spell, carefully

and correctly. The tray shrank at once. They were left kneeling on the floor looking at a reasonable-sized supper laid neatly in the centre of the table. "We might as well eat it," he said.

Angelica annoyed him thoroughly again by saying, as she picked up her spoon, "Well, I'm glad to know I'm not the only person who gets my spells wrong."

"I know I got it right," Tonino muttered into his spoon, but Angelica chose not to hear.

After a while, he was even more annoyed to find, every time he looked up, that Angelica was staring at him curiously. "What's the matter now?" he said at last, quite exasperated.

"I was waiting to see your filthy eating habits," she said. "But I think you must be on your best behaviour."

"I always eat like this!" Tonino saw that he had wound far too much spaghetti on his fork. He hurriedly unwound it.

The bulge of Angelica's forehead was wavy with frown-lines. "No you don't. Montanas always eat disgustingly because of the way Old Ricardo Petrocchi made them eat their words."

"Don't talk nonsense," said Tonino. "Anyway, it was Old Francesco Montana who made the Petrocchis eat *their* words."

"It was not!" Angelica said heatedly. "It was the first story I ever learnt. The Petrocchis made the Montanas eat their spells disguised as spaghetti."

"No they didn't. It was the other way round!" said Tonino. "It was the first story I ever learnt too."

Somehow, neither of them felt like finishing their spaghetti. They laid their forks down and went on arguing.

"And because of eating those spells," said Angelica, "the Montanas went quite disgusting and started eating their uncles and aunts when they died."

"We do not!" said Tonino. "You eat babies."

"How dare you!" said Angelica. "You eat cowpats for pizzas, and you can smell the Casa Montana right on the Corso."

"The Casa Petrocchi smells all down the Via Sant' Angelo," said Tonino, "and you can hear the flies buzzing from the New Bridge. You have babies like kittens and—"

"That's a lie!" shrieked Angelica. "You just put that about because you don't want people to know that the Montanas never get married properly!"

"Yes we do!" bawled Tonino. "It's you who don't!"

"I like that!" yelled Angelica. "I'll have you know, my brother got married, in church, just after Christmas. So there!"

"I don't believe you," said Tonino. "And my sister's going to get married in Spring, so—"

"I was a *bridesmaid*!" screamed Angelica.

While they argued, the tray quietly floated off the table and vanished somewhere near the windows. Tonino and Angelica looked irritably round for it, extremely annoyed that they had once again missed noticing how it got in and out.

"Now look what you've done!" said Angelica.

"It's your fault for telling lies about my family," said Tonino.

CHAPTER NINE

✳

"**I**f you're not careful," said Angelica, glowering under the bulge of her forehead, "I shall sing the first spell that comes into my head. And I hope it turns you into a slug."

That was a threat indeed. Tonino quailed a little. But the honour of the Montanas was at stake. "Take back what you said about my family," he said.

"Only if you take back what you said about mine," said Angelica. "Swear by the Angel of Caprona that none of those dreadful lies are true. Look. I've got the Angel here. Come and swear." Her pink finger jabbed down at the table top. She reminded Tonino of his school teacher on a bad day.

He left his creaking chair and leant over to see what she

was pointing at. Angelica fussily dusted away a shower of yellow varnish to show him that she indeed had the Angel, scratched with the useless tap into the top of the table. It was quite a good drawing, considering that the tap was not a good gouge and had shown a tendency to slip about. But Tonino was not prepared to admire it. "You've forgotten the scroll," he said.

Angelica jumped up, and her flimsy chair crashed over backwards. "That does it! You've asked for it!" She marched over to the empty space by the windows and took up a position of power. From there, with her hands raised, she looked at Tonino to see if he was going to relent. Tonino would have liked to relent. He did not want to be a slug. He sought about in his mind for some way of giving in which did not look like cowardice. But, as with everything, he was too slow. Angelica flounced round, so that her arms were no longer at quite the right angle.

"Right," she said. "I shall make it a cancel-spell, to cancel you out." And she began to sing.

Angelica's voice was horrible, sharp and flat by turns, and wandering from key to key. Tonino would have liked to interrupt her, or at least distract her by making noises, but he did not quite dare. That might only make things worse.

He waited while Angelica squawked out a couple of verses of a spell which seemed to centre round the words *turn the spell round, break the spell off.* Since he was a boy and not a spell, Tonino rather hoped it would not do anything to him.

Angelica raised her arms higher for the third verse and changed key for the sixth time. "Turn the spell off, break the spell round—"

"That's wrong," said Tonino.

"Don't you dare put me off!" snapped Angelica, and turned round to say it, which sent the angle of her arms more thoroughly wrong than ever. One hand was now pointing at a window. "I command the unbinding of that which was bound," she sang, cross and shrill.

Tonino looked quickly down at himself, but he seemed to be still there, and the usual colour. He told himself that he had known all along that such a bungled spell could not possibly work.

There came a great creaking from the ceiling, just above the windows. The whole room swayed. Then, to Tonino's amazement, the entire front wall of the room, windows and all, split away from the side walls and the ceiling, and fell outwards with a soft clatter – a curiously soft sound for the whole side of a house. A draught of musty-smelling air blew in through the open space.

Angelica was quite as astonished as Tonino. But that did not prevent her turning to him with a smug and triumphant smile. "See? My spells always work."

"Let's get out," said Tonino. "Quick. Before somebody comes."

They ran out across the painted panels between the windows, across the marks Tonino had made with the chair. They stepped down off the surprisingly clean, straight edge, where the wall had joined the ceiling, on to the terrace in front of the house. It appeared to be made of wood, not of stone as Tonino had expected. And beyond that—

They stopped, just in time, at the edge of a huge cliff. Both of them swayed forward, and caught at one another. The cliff went down sheer, into murky darkness. They could not see the bottom. Nor could they see much more when they looked straight ahead. There was a blaze of red-gold sunlight there, dazzling them.

"There's still a spell on the view," said Tonino.

"In that case," said Angelica, "let's just keep walking. There must be a road or a garden that we can't see."

There certainly should have been something of the kind, but it neither felt nor looked like that. Tonino was sure he could sense vast hollow spaces below the cliff. There were no city sounds, and only a strangely musty smell.

"Coward!" said Angelica.

"You go," said Tonino.

"Only if you go too," she said.

They hovered, glaring at one another. And, as they hovered, the blaze of sunlight was cut off by an immense black shape. "*Naughty!*" said a vast voice. "Bad children shall be punished."

A force almost too strong to feel swept them away on to the fallen wall. The fallen wall rose briskly back into its place, sweeping Angelica and Tonino with it, helplessly sliding and rolling, until they thumped on to the painted carpet. By that time, Tonino was so breathless and dizzy that he hardly heard the wall snap back into place with a click.

After that, the dizziness grew worse. Tonino knew he was in the grip of another spell. He struggled against it furiously, but whoever was casting it was immensely strong. He felt surging and bumping. The light from the windows changed, and changed again. Almost he could have sworn, the room was being *carried*. It stopped with a jolt. He heard Angelica's voice gabbling a prayer to Our Lady, and he did not blame her. Then there was a mystifying gap in what Tonino knew.

He came to himself because whoever was casting the spell wanted him to. Tonino was quite sure of that. The punishment would not be so much fun, unless Tonino knew about it.

He was in a confusion of light and noise – there was a huge blur of it to one side – and he was racing up and down a narrow wooden platform, dragging (of all things!) a string of sausages. He was wearing a bright red nightgown and there was a heaviness on the front of his face. Each time he reached one end of the wooden platform, he found a white cardboard dog there, with a frill round its neck. The dog's cardboard mouth opened and shut. It was making feeble cardboard attempts to get the sausages.

The noise was terrific. Tonino seemed to be making some of it himself. "What a clever fellow! What a clever fellow!" he heard himself squawking, in a voice quite unlike his own. It was like the noise you make singing into paper over a comb. The rest of the noise was coming from the lighted space to one side. Vast voices were roaring and laughing, mixed with tinny music.

"This is a dream!" Tonino told himself. But he knew it was not. He had a fair idea what was happening, though his head still felt muzzy and his eyes were blurred. As he raced back down the little platform, he turned his bleary eyes inwards, towards the heaviness on his face. Sure enough, blurred and doubled, he could see a great red and pink nose there. He was Mr Punch.

Naturally, then, he tried to dig in his heels and stop racing up and down, and to lift his hand and wrench off the huge pink nose. He could not do either. More than that, whoever was making him be Mr Punch promptly took mean pleasure in making him run faster and whirl the sausages about harder.

"Oh, very good!" yelled someone from the lighted space.

Tonino thought he knew that voice. He sped toward the cardboard Dog Toby again, whirled the sausages away from its cardboard jaws and waited for his head and eyes to stop feeling so fuzzy. He was sure they would. The mean person wanted him conscious. "What a clever fellow!" he squawked. As he raced down the stage the other way, he snatched a look across his huge nose towards the lighted space, but it was a blur. So he snatched a look towards the other side.

He saw the wall of a golden villa there, with four long windows. Beside each window stood a little dark cypress tree. Now he knew why the strange room had seemed so shoddy. It was only meant as scenery. The door on the outside wall was painted on. Between the villa and the stage was a hole. The person who was working the puppets ought to have been down there, but Tonino could only see empty blackness. It was all being done by magic.

Just then he was distracted by a cardboard person diving upwards from the hole, squawking that Mr Punch had stolen his sausages. Tonino was forced to stand still and squawk back. He was glad of a rest by then. Meanwhile, the cardboard dog seized the sausages and dived out of sight with them. The audience clapped and shouted, "Look at Dog Toby!" The cardboard person sped past Tonino squawking that he would fetch the police.

Once again, Tonino tried to look out at the audience. This time, he could dimly see a brightly lit room and black bulky shapes sitting in chairs, but it was like trying to see something against the sun. His eyes watered. A tear ran down the pink beak on his face. And Tonino could feel that the mean person was delighted to see that. He thought Tonino was crying. Tonino was annoyed, but also rather pleased; it looked as if the person could be fooled by his own mean thoughts. He stared out, in spite of the dazzle, trying to see the mean person, but all he could clearly see was a carving up near the roof of the lighted room. It was the Angel of Caprona, one hand held out in blessing, the other holding the scroll.

Then he was jumped round to face Judy. On the other side of him, the wall had gone from the front of the villa. The scene was the room he knew only too well, with the chandelier artistically alight.

Judy was coming along the stage holding the white rolled-up shape of the baby. Judy wore a blue nightdress and a blue cap. Her face was mauve, with a nose in the middle of it nearly as large and red as Tonino's. But the eyes on either side of it were Angelica's, alternately blinking and wide with terror. She blinked beseechingly at Tonino as she squawked, "I have to go out, Mr Punch. Mind you mind the baby!"

"Don't want to mind the baby!" he squawked.

All through the long silly conversation, he could see Angelica's eyes blinking at him, imploring him to think of a spell to stop this. But of course Tonino could not. He did not think Rinaldo, or even Antonio, could stop anything as powerful as this. Angel of Caprona! he thought. Help us! That made him feel better, although nothing stopped the spell. Angelica planted the baby in his arms and dived out of sight.

The baby started to cry. Tonino first squawked abuse at it, then took it by the end of its long white dress and beat its brains out on the platform. The baby was much more realistic than Dog Toby. It may have been only cardboard, but it wriggled and waved its arms and cried most horribly. Tonino could almost have believed it was Cousin Claudia's baby. It so horrified him that he found he was repeating the words of the *Angel of Caprona* as he swung the baby up and down. And those might not have been the right words, but he could feel they were doing something. When he finally flung the white bundle over the front of the stage, he could see the shiny floor the baby fell on, away below. And when he looked up at the clapping spectators, he could see them too, equally clearly.

The first person he saw was the Duke of Caprona. He was sitting on a gilded chair, in a glitter of buttons, laughing gigantically. Tonino wondered how he could laugh like that at something so horrible, until he remembered that he had stood himself, a score of times, and laughed himself sick, at just the same thing. But those had been only puppets. Then it dawned on Tonino that the Duke thought they *were* puppets. He was laughing at the skill of the showman.

"What a clever fellow!" squawked Tonino, and was made to dance about gleefully, without wanting to in the least. But as he danced, he looked sharply at the rest of the audience, to see who it was who knew he was not a puppet.

To his terror, a good half of them knew. Tonino met a knowing look on the faces of the three grave men surrounding the Duke, and the same on the elegantly made-up faces of the two ladies with the Duchess. And the Duchess – as soon as Tonino saw the amused arch of the Duchess's eyebrows and the little, secret smile on her mouth, he knew she was the one doing it. He looked her in the eyes. Yes, she was an enchantress. That was what had so troubled him about her when he saw her before. And the Duchess saw him look, and smiled less secretly, because Tonino could do nothing about it.

That really frightened Tonino. But Angelica came swooping upwards again, with a large stick clutched in her arms, and he had no time to think.

"What have you done with the baby?" squawked Angelica. And she belaboured Tonino with the stick. It really hurt. It knocked him to his knees and went on bashing at him. Tonino could see Angelica's lips moving. Though her silly squeaky voice kept saying, "I'll teach you to kill the baby!" her mouth was forming the words of the *Angel of Caprona*. That was because she knew what came next.

Tonino said the words of the *Angel* too and tried to stay crouched on the floor. But it was no good. He was made to spring up, wrest the stick from Judy and beat Angelica with it. He could see the Duke laughing, and the courtiers smiling. The Duchess's smile was very broad now, because, of course, Tonino was going to have to beat Angelica to death.

Tonino tried to hold the stick so that it would only hit Angelica lightly. She might be a Petrocchi and a thoroughly irritating girl, but she had not deserved this. But the stick leapt up and down of its own accord, and Tonino's arms went with it. Angelica fell on her knees and then on her face. Her squawks redoubled, as Tonino smote away at her back, and then her voice stopped. She lay with her head hanging down from the front of the platform, looking just like a puppet. Tonino found himself having to kick her down the empty space between the false villa and the stage. He heard the distant *flop* as she fell. And then he was forced to skip and cackle with glee, while the Duchess threw back her head and laughed as heartily as the Duke.

Tonino hated her. He was so angry and so miserable that he did not mind at all when a cardboard policeman appeared and he chased him with the stick too. He laid into the policeman as if he was the Duchess and not a cardboard doll at all.

"Are you all right, Lucrezia?" he heard the Duke say.

Tonino looked sideways as he dealt another mighty swipe at the policeman's cardboard helmet. He saw the Duchess wince as the stick landed. He was not surprised when the policeman was immediately whisked away and he himself forced into a violent capering and even louder squawking. He let himself do it. He felt truly gleeful as he squawked, "What a clever fellow!" for what felt like the thousandth time. For he understood what had happened. The Duchess *was* the policeman, in a sort of way. She was putting some of herself into all the puppets to make them work. But he must not let her know he knew. Tonino capered and chortled, doing his best to seem terrified, and kept his eyes on that carving of the Angel, high up over the door of the room.

And now the hooded Hangman-puppet appeared, dragging a little wooden gibbet with a string noose dangling from it. Tonino capered cautiously. This was where the Duchess did for him unless he was very careful. On the other hand, if this Punch and Judy show went as it should, he might just do for the Duchess.

The silly scene began. Tonino had never worked so hard at anything in his life. He kept repeating the words of the *Angel* in his head, both as a kind of prayer and as a smoke-screen, so that the Duchess would not understand what he was trying to do. At the same time, he thought, fiercely and vengefully, that the Hangman was not just a puppet – it was the Duchess herself. And, also at the same time, he attended to Mr Punch's conversation with all his might. This had to go right.

"Come along, Mr Punch," croaked the Hangman. "Just put your head in this noose."

"How do I do that?" asked Mr Punch and Tonino, both pretending hard to be stupid.

"You put your head in here," croaked the Hangman, putting one hand through the noose.

Mr Punch and Tonino, both of them quivering with cunning, put his head first one side of the noose, then the other. "Is this right? Is this?" Then, pretending even harder to be stupid, "I can't see how to do it. You'll have to show me."

Either the Duchess was wanting to play with Tonino's feelings, or she was trying the same cunning. They went through this several times. Each time, the Hangman put his hand through the noose to show Mr Punch what to do. Tonino did not dare look at the Duchess. He looked at the Hangman and kept thinking, That's the Duchess, and reciting the *Angel* for all he was worth. At last, to his relief, the Duke became restive.

"Come on, Mr Punch!" he shouted.

"You'll have to put your head in and show me," Mr Punch and Tonino said, as persuasively as he knew how.

"Oh well," croaked the Hangman. "Since you're so stupid." And he put his cardboard head through the noose.

Mr Punch and Tonino promptly pulled the rope and hanged him. But Tonino thought, This is the *Duchess*! and went as limp and heavy as he could. For just a second, his full puppet's weight swung on the end of the rope.

It only lasted that second. Tonino had a glimpse of the Duchess on her feet with her hands to her throat. He felt real triumph. Then he was thrown, flat on his face, across the stage, unable to move at all. There he was forced to lie. His head hung down from the front of the stage, so that he could see very little. But he gathered that the Duchess was being led tenderly away, with the Duke fussing round her.

I think I feel as pleased as Punch, he thought.

CHAPTER TEN

✳

*P*aolo never wanted to remember that night afterwards. He was still staring at the sick yellow message in the yard, when the rest of the family arrived. He was crowded aside to let Old Niccolo and Aunt Francesca through, but Benvenuto spat at them like hot fat hitting fire and would not let them pass.

"Let be, old boy," Old Niccolo said. "You've done your best." He turned to Aunt Francesca. "I shall never forgive the Petrocchis," he said. "Never."

Paolo was once again struck by how wretched and goblin-like his grandfather looked. He had thought Old Niccolo was helping vast, panting, muddy Aunt Francesca along, but he now wondered if it was not the other way round.

"Well. Let's get rid of this horrible message," Old Niccolo said irritably to the rest of them.

He raised his arms to start the family on the spell and collapsed. His hands went to his chest. He slid to his knees, and his face was a strange colour. Paolo thought he was dead until he saw him breathing, in uneven jerks. Elizabeth, Uncle Lorenzo and Aunt Maria rushed to him.

"Heart attack," Uncle Lorenzo said, nodding over at Antonio. "Get that spell going. We've got to get him indoors."

"Paolo, run for the doctor," said Elizabeth.

As Paolo ran, he heard the burst of singing behind him. When he came back with the doctor, the message had vanished and Old Niccolo had been carried up to bed. Aunt Francesca, still muddy, with her hair hanging down one side, was roving up and down the yard like a moving mountain, crying and wringing her hands.

"Spells are forbidden," she called out to Paolo. "I've stopped everything."

"And a good thing too!" the doctor said sourly. "A man of Niccolo Montana's age has no business to be brawling in the streets. And make your great-aunt lie down," he said to Paolo. "She'll be in bed next."

Aunt Francesca would only go to the Saloon, where she refused even to sit down. She raged up and down, wailing about Old Niccolo, weeping about Tonino, declaring that the virtue had gone from the Casa Montana for good, and uttering terrible threats against the Petrocchis. Nobody else was much better. The children cried with tiredness. Elizabeth and the aunts worried about Old Niccolo, and then about Aunt Francesca. In the Scriptorium, among all the abandoned spells, Antonio and the uncles sat rigid with worry, and the rest of the Casa was full of older cousins wandering about and cursing the Petrocchis.

Paolo found Rinaldo leaning moodily on the gallery rail, in spite of it being dark now and really quite cold. "Curse those Petrocchis," he said gloomily to Paolo. "We can't even earn a living now, let alone help if there's a war."

Paolo, in spite of his misery, was very flattered that Rinaldo seemed to think him old enough to talk family business to. He said, "Yes, it's awful," and tried to lean on the rail in the same elegant attitude as Rinaldo. It was not easy, since Paolo was not nearly tall enough, but he leant and prepared the arguments he would use to persuade Rinaldo that Tonino was in the hands of an enemy enchanter. That was not easy either. Paolo knew that Rinaldo would not listen to him if he dropped the least small hint that he had talked to a Petrocchi – and besides, he would have died rather than told his cousin. But he knew that, if he persuaded Rinaldo, Rinaldo would rescue Tonino in five dashing minutes. Rinaldo was a true Montana.

While he thought, Rinaldo said angrily, "What possessed that stupid brat Tonino to read that blessed book? I shall give him something to think about when we get him back!"

Paolo shivered in the cold. "Tonino always reads books." Then he shifted a bit – the elegant attitude was not at all comfortable – and asked timidly, "How shall we get him back?"

This was not at all what he had planned to say. He was annoyed with himself.

"What's the use?" Rinaldo said. "We know where he is – in the Casa Petrocchi. And if he's uncomfortable there, it's his own fault!"

"But he's not!" Paolo protested. As far as he could see in the light from the yard lamp, Rinaldo turned and looked at him jeeringly. The discussion seemed to be getting further from the way he had planned it every second. "An enemy enchanter's got him," he said. "The one Chrestomanci talked about."

Rinaldo laughed. "Load of old crab-apples, Paolo. Our friend had been talking to the Petrocchis. He invented his convenient enchanter because he wanted us all working for Caprona. Most of us saw through it at once."

"Then who made that mist on the Corso?" Paolo said. "It wasn't us, and it wasn't them."

But Rinaldo only said, "Who said it wasn't them?"

As Paolo could not say it was Renata Petrocchi, he could not answer. Instead, he said rather desperately, "Come with me to the Casa Petrocchi. If you used a finding-spell, you could *prove* Tonino isn't there."

"What?" Rinaldo seemed astounded. "What kind of fool do you take me for, Paolo? I'm not going to take on a whole family of spell-makers single-handed. And if I go there and use a spell, and they do something to Tonino, everyone's going to blame me, aren't they? For something we know anyway. It's not worth it, Paolo. But I tell you what—"

He was interrupted by Aunt Gina trumpeting below in

the yard. "Notti's is the only chemist open by now. Tell him it's for Niccolo Montana!"

With some relief, Paolo dropped the elegant attitude entirely and leant over the rail to watch Lucia and Corinna hurry through the yard with the doctor's prescription. The sight gave his stomach a wrench of worry. "Do you think Old Niccolo's going to die, Rinaldo?"

Rinaldo shrugged. "Could be. He's pretty old. It's about time the old idiot gave up anyway. I shall be one step closer to being head of the Casa Montana then."

A peculiar thing happened inside Paolo's head then. He had never given much thought to who might follow Antonio – for it was clear his father would follow Old Niccolo – as head of the Casa Montana. But he had never, for some reason, thought it might be Rinaldo. Now he tried to imagine Rinaldo doing the things Old Niccolo did. And as soon as he did, he saw Rinaldo was quite unsuitable. Rinaldo was vain, and selfish – and cowardly, provided he could be a coward and still keep up a good appearance. It was as if Rinaldo had said a powerful spell to clear Paolo's eyes.

It never occurred to Rinaldo, expert spell-maker though he was, that a few ordinary words could make such a difference. He bent towards Paolo and dropped his voice to a melodious murmur. "I was going to tell you, Paolo. I'm going round enlisting all the young ones. We're going to swear to work a secret revenge on the Petrocchis. We'll do something worse than make them eat their words. Are you with me? Will you swear to join the plan?"

Maybe he was in earnest. It would suit Rinaldo to work

in secret, with lots of willing helpers. But Paolo was sure that this plan was a step in Rinaldo's plans to be head of the Casa. Paolo sidled away along the rail.

"Are you game?" Rinaldo whispered, laughing a little.

Paolo sidled beyond grabbing-distance. "Tell you later." He turned and scudded away. Rinaldo laughed and did not try to catch him. He thought Paolo was scared.

Paolo went down into the yard, feeling more lonely than he had felt in his life. Tonino was not there. Tonino was not vain, or selfish, or cowardly. And nobody would help him find Tonino. Paolo had not noticed until now how much he depended on Tonino. They did everything important together. Even if Paolo was busy on his own, he knew Tonino was there somewhere, sitting reading, ready to put his book down if Paolo needed him. Now there seemed to be nothing for Paolo to do. And the whole Casa reeked of worry.

He went to the kitchen, where there seemed, at last, to be something happening. All his small cousins were there. Rosa and Marco were trying to make soup for them.

"Come in and help, Paolo," Rosa said. "We're going to put them to bed after soup, but we're having a bit of trouble."

Both she and Marco were looking tired and flustered. Most of the little ones were grizzling, including the baby. The trouble was Lucia's spell. Paolo understood this because Marco dumped the baby in his arms. Its wrapper was covered with orange grease. "Yuk!" said Paolo.

"I know," said Rosa. "Well, Marco, better try again. Clean saucepan. Clean water. The very last packet of soup-powder – don't make that face, Paolo. We've got through all the vegetables. They just sail away to the waste-bins, and they're mouldy before they get there."

Paolo looked nervously at the door, wondering if the enemy enchanter was powerful enough to overhear him. "Try a cancel-spell," he whispered.

"Aunt Gina went through them all this afternoon," said Rosa. "No good. Little Lucia used the *Angel of Caprona*, you see. We're trying Marco's way now. Ready, Marco?"

Rosa opened the packet of soup and held it over the saucepan. As the dry pink powder poured into the water, Marco leant over the saucepan and sang furiously. Paolo watched them nervously. This was just what the message told them not to do, he was sure. When all the powder was in the water, Rosa and Marco peered anxiously into the saucepan. "Have we done it?" asked Marco.

"I think—" Rosa began, and ended in a yell of exasperation. "Oh *no*!" The little pasta shells in the powder had turned into real sea-shells, little grey ones. "With *creatures* in!" Rosa said despairingly, dipping a spoonful out. "Where *is* Lucia?" she said. "Bring her here. Tell her I— No, don't. Just fetch her, Paolo."

"She's gone to the chemist," said Paolo.

There was shouting in the yard. Paolo passed the greasy baby to the nearest cousin and shot outside, dreading another sick yellow message about Tonino. Or there was just a chance the noise was Lucia.

It was neither. It was Rinaldo. The uncles must have

left the Scriptorium, for Rinaldo was making a bonfire of spells in the middle of the yard. Domenico, Carlo and Luigi were busily carrying armfuls of scrips, envelopes and scrolls down from the gallery. Paolo recognised, already curling among the flames, the army-charms he and the other children had spent such a time copying. It was a shocking waste of work.

"This is what the Petrocchis have forced us to!" shouted Rinaldo, striking an attitude beside the flames. It was evidently part of his plan to enlist the young ones.

Paolo was glad to see Antonio and Uncle Lorenzo hurry out of the Saloon.

"Rinaldo!" shouted Antonio. "Rinaldo, we're worried about Umberto. We want you to go to the University and enquire."

"Send Domenico," said Rinaldo, and turned back to the flames.

"No," said Antonio. "You go." There was something about the way he said it that caused Rinaldo to back away from him.

"I'll go," said Rinaldo. He held up one hand, laughing. "I was only joking, Uncle Antonio."

He left at once. "Take those spells back," Uncle Lorenzo said to the other three cousins. "I hate to see good work wasted." Domenico, Carlo and Luigi obeyed without a word. Antonio and Uncle Lorenzo went to the bonfire and tried to stamp out the flames, but they were burning too strongly. Paolo saw them look at one another, rather guiltily, and then lean forward and whisper a spell over the fire. It flicked out as if it had been turned off with a switch. Paolo sighed worriedly. It was plain that no one in the Casa Montana could drop the habit of using spells. He wondered how long it would be before the enemy enchanter noticed.

"Fetch a light!" Antonio shouted to Domenico. "And sort out the ones that aren't burnt."

Paolo went back to the kitchen before they asked him to help. The bonfire had given him an idea.

"There is quite a bit of mince," Rosa was saying. "Dare we try with that?"

"Why don't you," said Paolo, "take the food to the dining room? I'll light a fire there, and you can cook it on that."

"The boy's a genius!" said Marco.

They did that. Rosa cooked by relays and Marco made cocoa. The children were fed first, Paolo included. Paolo sat on one of the long benches, thinking it was almost enjoyable – except if he thought of Tonino, or Old Niccolo in bed upstairs. He was very pleased and surprised when a sudden bundle of claw and warm-iron muscle landed on his knee. Benvenuto was missing Tonino too. He rubbed against Paolo with a kind of desperation, but he would not purr.

Rosa and Marco were getting up to put the young ones to bed, when there was a sudden great clanging, outside in the night.

"Good Heavens!" said Rosa, and opened the yard door.

The noise flooded in, an uneven metal sound, hasty and huge. The nearest – *clang-clang-clang* – was so near that it could only be the bell of Sant' Angelo's. Behind it, the bell of the Cathedral tolled. And beyond that, now near, now faint and tinny, every bell in every church in Caprona beat and boomed and clashed and chimed. Corinna and Lucia came racing in, their faces bright with cold excitement.

"We're at war! The Duke's declared war!"

Marco said he thought he had better go. "Oh no, don't!" Rosa cried out. "Not yet. By the way, Lucia—"

Lucia took a quick look at the cooking in the hearth. "I'll go and take Aunt Gina the prescription," she said, and prudently ran away.

Marco and Rosa looked at one another. "Three States against us and no spells to fight with," said Marco. "We're not likely to have a long and happy marriage, are we?"

"Mr Notti says the Final Reserve is being called up tomorrow," Corinna said encouragingly. She caught Rosa's eye. "Come on, you kids," she said to four cousins at random. "Bedtime."

While the young ones were being put to bed, Paolo sat nursing Benvenuto, feeling more dismal than ever. He wondered if there would be soldiers from Florence and Pisa and Siena in Caprona by tomorrow. Would guns fire in the streets? He thought of big marble chips shot off the Cathedral, the New Bridge broken, despite all the spells in it, and swarthy enemy soldiers dragging Rosa off screaming. And he saw that all this could really have happened by the end of the week.

Here, he became quite certain that Benvenuto was trying to tell him something. He could tell from the accusing stare of Benvenuto's yellow eyes. But he simply could not understand.

"I'll try," he said to Benvenuto. "I really will try."

He had, fleetingly, the feeling that Benvenuto was glad. Encouraged by this, Paolo bent his head and stared at Benvenuto's urgent face. But it did no good. All that Paolo could get out of it was a picture in his mind – a picture of somewhere with a coloured marble front, very large and beautiful.

"The Church of Sant' Angelo?" he said doubtfully.

While Benvenuto's tail was still lashing with annoyance, Rosa and Marco came back. "Oh dear!" Rosa said to Marco. "There's Paolo taking all the troubles of the Casa on his shoulders again!"

Paolo looked up in surprise.

Marco said, "You look just like Antonio sometimes."

"I can't understand Benvenuto," Paolo said despairingly.

Marco sat on the table beside him. "Then he'll have to find some other way of telling us what he wants," he said. "He's a clever cat – the cleverest I've ever known. He'll do it."

He put out a hand and Benvenuto let him stroke his head. "Your ears," said Marco, "Sir Cat, are like sea-holly without the prickles."

Rosa perched on the table too, on the other side of Paolo. "What is it, Paolo? Tonino?"

Paolo nodded. "Nobody will believe me that the enemy enchanter's got him."

"We do," said Marco.

Rosa said, "Paolo, it's just as well he's got Tonino and not you. Tonino'll take it much more calmly."

Paolo was a little bewildered. "Why do you two believe in the enchanter and no one else does?"

"What makes you think he exists?" Marco countered.

Even to Rosa and Marco, Paolo could not bring himself to tell of his embarrassing encounter with a Petrocchi. "There was a horrible fog at the end of the fight," he said.

Rosa and Marco jumped round delightedly. Their hands met with a smack over Paolo's head. "It worked! It worked!" And Marco added, "We were hoping someone would mention a certain fog! Did there seem to have been a large-scale cancel-spell with it, by any chance?"

"Yes," said Paolo.

"*We* made that fog," Rosa said. "Marco and me. We were hoping to stop the fighting, but it took us ages to make it, because all the magic in Caprona was going into the fight."

Paolo digested this. That took care of the one piece of proof that did not depend on the word of a Petrocchi. Perhaps the enchanter did not exist after all. Perhaps Tonino really was at the Casa Petrocchi. He remembered that Renata had not said Angelica was missing until the fog cleared and she knew who he was. "Look," he said. "Will you two come to the Casa Petrocchi with me and see if Tonino's there?"

He was aware that Rosa and Marco were exchanging some kind of look above his head.

"Why?" said Rosa.

"Because," said Paolo. "Because." The need to persuade

them cleared his wits at last. "Because Guido Petrocchi said Angelica Petrocchi was missing too."

"I'm afraid we can't," Marco said, with what sounded like real regret. "You'd understand, if you knew how pressing our reasons are, believe me!"

Paolo did not understand. He knew that, with these two, it was not cowardice, or pride, or anything like that. That only made it more maddening. "Oh, nobody will help!" he cried out.

Rosa put her arm around him. "Paolo! You're just like Father. You think you have to do everything yourself. There is one thing we can do."

"Call Chrestomanci?" said Marco.

Paolo felt Rosa nod. "But he's in Rome," he objected.

"It doesn't matter," said Marco. "He's that kind of enchanter. If he's near enough and you need him enough, he comes when you call."

"I must cook!" said Rosa, jumping off the table.

Just before the second supper was ready, Rinaldo came back, in great good spirits. Uncle Umberto and old Luigi Petrocchi had had another fight, in the dining-hall of the University. That was why Uncle Umberto had not turned up to see how Old Niccolo was. He and Luigi were both in bed, prostrated with exhaustion. Rinaldo had been drinking wine with some students who told him all about the fight. The students' supper had been ruined. Cutlets and pasta had flown about, followed by chairs, tables and benches. Umberto had tried to drown Luigi in a soup tureen, and Luigi had replied by hurling the whole of the Doctors' supper at Umberto. The students were going on strike. They did not mind the fight, but Luigi had shown them that the Doctors' food was better than theirs.

Paolo listened without truly attending. He was thinking about Tonino and wondering if he dared depend on the word of a Petrocchi.

CHAPTER ELEVEN

✴

After a while, someone came and picked Tonino up. That was unpleasant. His legs and arms dragged and dangled in all directions, and he could not do anything about it. He was plunged somewhere much darker. Then he was left to lie amid a great deal of bumping and scraping, as if he were in a box which was being pushed across a floor. When it stopped, he found he could move. He sat up, trembling all over.

He was in the same room as before, but it seemed to be much smaller. He could tell that, if he stood up, his head would brush the little lighted chandelier in the ceiling. So he was larger now; where he had been three inches tall before, he must now be more like nine. The puppets must be too big for their scenery, and the false villa meant to look as if it was some distance away. And, with the Duchess suddenly taken ill, none of her helpers had bothered what size Tonino was. They had simply made sure he was shut up again.

"Tonino," whispered Angelica.

Tonino whirled round. Half the room was full of a pile of lax puppet bodies. He scanned the cardboard head of the policeman, then his enemy the Hangman, and the white sausage of the baby, and came upon Angelica's face halfway up the pile. It was her own face, though swollen and tearstained. Tonino clapped his hand to his nose. To his relief, the red beak was gone, though he still seemed to be wearing Mr Punch's scarlet nightgown.

"I'm sorry," he said. His teeth seemed to be chattering. "I tried not to hurt you. Are your bones broken?"

"No–o," said Angelica. She did not sound too sure. "Tonino, what happened?"

"I hanged the Duchess," Tonino said, and he felt some vicious triumph as he said it. "I didn't kill her though," he added regretfully.

Angelica laughed. She laughed until the heap of puppets was shaking and sliding about. But Tonino could not find it funny. He burst into tears, even though he was crying in front of a Petrocchi.

"Oh dear," said Angelica. "Tonino, stop it! Tonino – please!" She struggled out from among the puppets and hobbled looming through the room. Her head banged the chandelier and sent it tinkling and casting mad shadows over them as she knelt down beside Tonino. "Tonino, please stop. She'll be furious as soon as she feels better."

Angelica was wearing Judy's blue cap and Judy's blue dress still. She took off the blue cap and held it out to Tonino. "Here. Blow on that. I used the baby's dress. It made me feel better." She tried to smile at him, but the smile went hopelessly crooked in her swollen face. Angelica's large forehead must have hit the floor first. It was now enlarged by a huge red bump. Under it, the grin looked grotesque.

Tonino understood it was meant for a smile and smiled back, as well as he could for his chattering teeth.

"Here." Angelica loomed back through the room to the pile of puppets and heaved at the Hangman. She returned with his black felt cape. "Put this on."

Tonino wrapped himself in the cape and blew his nose on the blue cap and felt better.

Angelica heaved more puppets about. "I'm going to wear the policeman's jacket," she said. "Tonino – have you thought?"

"Not really," said Tonino. "I sort of know."

He had known from the moment he looked at the Duchess. She was the enchanter who was sapping the strength of Caprona and spoiling the spells of the Casa Montana. Tonino was not sure about the Duke – probably he was too stupid to count. But in spite of the Duchess's enchantments, the spells of the Casa Montana – and the Casa Petrocchi – must still be strong enough to be a nuisance to her. So he and Angelica had been kidnapped to blackmail both houses into stopping making spells. And if they stopped, Caprona would be defeated. The frightening part was that Tonino and Angelica were the only two people who knew, and the Duchess did not care that they knew. It was not only that even someone as clever as Paolo would never think of looking in the Palace, inside a Punch and Judy show: it must mean that the two of them would be dead before anyone found them.

"We absolutely have to get away," said Angelica. "Before she's better from being hanged."

"She'll have thought of that," said Tonino.

"I'm not sure," said Angelica. "I could tell everyone was startled to death. They let me see you being put through the floor, and I think we could get out that way. It will be easier now we're bigger."

Tonino fastened the cape round him and struggled to his feet, though he felt almost too tired and bruised to bother. His head hit the chandelier too. Huge flickering shadows fled round the room, and made the heap of puppets look as if they were squirming about. "Where did they put me through?" he said.

"Just where you're standing," said Angelica.

Tonino backed against the windows and looked at the place. He would not have known there was any opening. But, now Angelica had told him, he could see, disguised by the painted swirls of the carpet and confused by the swinging light, the faintest black line. The outline made an oblong about the size of the shoddy dining-table. The tray of supper must have come through that way too.

"Sing an opening spell," Angelica commanded him.

"I don't know one," Tonino was forced to confess.

He could tell by the stiff way Angelica stood that she was trying not to say a number of nasty things. "Well, I don't dare," she said. "You saw what happened last time. If I do anything, they'll catch us again and punish us by making us be puppets. And I couldn't bear another time."

Tonino was not sure he could bear it either, even though, now he thought about it, he was not sure it had been a punishment. The Duchess had probably intended to make them perform anyway. She was quite mean enough. On the other hand, he was not sure he could stand another of Angelica's botched spells, either. "Well, it's only a trap-door," he said. "It must be held up by one of those little hooks. Let's try bashing at it with the candlesticks."

"And if there's a spell on it?" said Angelica. "Oh, come on. Let's try."

They seized a candlestick each and knelt beside the windows, knocking diligently at the scarcely-seen black line. The cardboard was tough and pulpy. The candlesticks shortly looked like metal weeping-willow trees. But they succeeded in making a crumbly hollow in the middle of one edge of the hidden door. Tonino thought he could see a glimmer of metal showing. He raised his bent candlestick high to deliver a mighty blow.

"*Stop!*" hissed Angelica.

There were large shuffling footsteps somewhere. Tonino lowered the candlestick by gentle fractions and scarcely dared breathe. A distant voice grumbled… "Mice then" … "Nothing here…" It was suddenly very much darker. Someone had switched off a light, leaving them only with the bluish glimmer of the little chandelier. The footsteps shuffled. A door bumped, and there was silence.

Angelica laid her candlestick down and began trying to tear at the cardboard with her fingers. Tonino got up and wandered away. It was no good. Someone was going to hear them, whatever they did. The Palace was full of footmen and soldiers. Tonino would have given up then and waited for the Duchess to do her worst. Only now he was standing up, the cardboard room seemed so small. Half of it was filled with the puppets. There was hardly room to move. Tonino wanted to hurl himself at the walls and scream. He did make a movement, and knocked the table. Because he was so much bigger and heavier now, the table swayed and creaked.

"I know!" he said. "Finish drawing the Angel."

The bump on Angelica's forehead turned up to him. "I'm not in the mood for doodling."

"Not a doodle, a spell," Tonino explained. "And then pull the table over us while we make a hole in the trap door."

Angelica did not need telling that the Angel was the most potent spell in Caprona. She threw the candlestick aside and scrambled up. "That might just work," she said. "You know, for a Montana, you have very good ideas." Her head hit the chandelier again. In the confusion of swinging shadows, they could not find the tap Angelica had been drawing with. Tonino had to jam his head and arm into the tiny bathroom and pull off the other useless tap.

Even when the shadows stopped swinging, the Angel scratched on the table was hard to see. It now looked faint and small.

"He needs his scroll," said Angelica. "And I'd better put in a halo to make sure he's holy."

Angelica was now so much bigger and stronger that she kept dropping the tap. The halo, when she had scratched it in, was too big, and the scroll would not go right. The table swayed this way and that, the tap ploughed and skidded, and there was a danger the Angel would end up a complete mess.

"It's so fiddly!" said Angelica. "Will that do?"

"No," said Tonino. "It needs the scroll more unrolled. Some of the words show on our Angel."

Because he was quite right, Angelica lost her temper. "All right! Do it yourself, if you're so clever, you horrible Montana!"

She held the tap out to Tonino and he snatched it from her, quite as angry. "Here," he said, ploughing up a long curl of varnish. "Here's the hanging bit. And the words go sideways. You can see *Carmen pa, Venit ang, Cap* and a lot more, but there won't be room for it."

"Our Angel," said Angelica, "says *cis saeculare, elus cantare* and *virtus data* near the end." Tonino scratched away and took no notice. It was hard enough shaping tiny letters with a thing like a tap, without listening to Angelica arguing. "Well it does!" said Angelica. "I've often wondered why it's not the words we sing—"

The same idea came to both of them. They stared at one another, nose to nose across the scratched varnish.

"*Finding* the words means *looking* for them," said Tonino.

"And they were over our gates all the time! Oh how *stupid*!" exclaimed Angelica. "Come on. We *must* get out now!"

Tonino left the scroll with *Carmen* scraped on it. There was really no room for any more. They dragged the creaking, swaying table across the hole they had made in the floor and set to work underneath it, hacking lumps out of the painted floor.

Shortly, they could see a bar of silvery metal stretching from the trap door to the floor underneath them. Tonino forced the end of his candlestick down between the battered cardboard edges and heaved sideways at the metal.

"There's a spell on it," he said.

"Angel of Caprona," Angelica said at the same moment.

And the bar slipped sideways. A big oblong piece of the floor dropped away from in front of their knees and swung, leaving a very deep dark hole.

"Let's get the Hangman's rope," said Angelica.

They edged along to the pile of puppets and disentangled the string from the little gibbet. Tonino tied it to the table leg.

"It's a long way down," he said dubiously.

"It's only a few feet *really*," Angelica said. "And we're not heavy enough to hurt. I went all floppy when you kicked me off the stage and – well – I didn't break anything anyway."

Tonino let Angelica go first, swinging down into the dark space like an energetic blue monkey. *Crunch* went the shoddy table. *Creeeak*. And it swayed towards the leg where the rope was tied.

"Angel of Caprona!" Tonino whispered.

The table plunged, one corner first, down into the space. The cardboard room rattled. And, with a rending and creaking of wood, the table stuck, mostly in the hole, but with one corner out and wedged against the sides. There was a thump from below. Tonino was fairly sure he was stuck in the room for good now.

"I'm down," Angelica whispered up. "You can pull the rope up. It nearly reaches the floor."

Tonino leaned over and fumbled the string up from the table leg. He was sure there had been a miracle. That leg ought to have broken off, or the table ought to have gone down the hole. He whispered, "Angel of Caprona!" again as he slid down under the table into the dark.

The table creaked hideously, but it held together. The string burnt Tonino's hands as he slid, and then it was suddenly not there. His feet hit the floor almost at once.

"Oof!" he went. His feet felt as if they had been knocked up through his legs.

Down there, they were standing on the shiny floor of a Palace room. The towering walls of the Punch and Judy show were on three sides of them. Instead of a back wall, there was a curtain, intended to hide the puppet-master, and very dim light was coming in round its edges. They pulled one end of the curtain aside. It felt coarse and heavy, like a sack. Behind it was the wall of the room. The puppet show had evidently been simply pushed away to one side. There was just space for

Angelica and Tonino to squeeze past the ends of the show, into a large room lit by moonlight falling in strong silver blocks across its shiny floor.

It was the same room where the court had watched the Punch and Judy show. The puppet show had not been put away. Tonino thought of the time he and Angelica had tottered on the edge of the stage, looking into nothingness. They could have been killed. That seemed another miracle. Then, they must have been in some kind of storeroom. But, when the Duchess was so mysteriously taken ill, no one had bothered to put them back there.

The moonlight glittered on the polished face of the Angel, high up on the other side of the room, leaning out over some big double doors. There were other doors, but Tonino and Angelica set out, without hesitation, towards the Angel. Both of them took it for a guide.

"Oh bother!" said Angelica, before they reached the first block of moonlight. "We're still small. I thought we'd be the right size as soon as we got out, didn't you?"

Tonino's one idea was to get out, whatever his size. "It'll be easier to hide like this," he said. "Someone in your Casa can easily turn you back." He pulled the Hangman's cloak round him and shivered. It was colder out in the big room. He could see the moon through the big windows, riding high and cold in a wintry dark blue sky. It was not going to be fun running through the streets in a red nightgown.

"But I *hate* being this small!" Angelica complained. "We'll never be able to get down stairs."

She was right to complain, as Tonino soon discovered.

It seemed a mile across the polished floor. When they reached the double doors, they were tired out. High above them, the carved Angel dangled a scroll they could not possibly read, and no longer looked so friendly. But the doors were open a crack. They managed to push the crack wider by leaning their backs against the edge of both doors. It was maddening to think they could have opened them with one hand if only they had been the proper size.

Beyond was an even bigger room. This one was full of chairs and small tables. The only advantage of being doll-sized was that they could walk under every piece of furniture in a straight line to the far-too-distant door. It was like trudging through a golden moonlit forest, where every tree had an elegant swan-bend to its trunk. The floor seemed to be marble.

Before they reached the door, they were quarrelling again from sheer tiredness.

"It's going to take all *night* to get out of here!" Angelica grumbled.

"Oh shut up!" said Tonino. "You make more fuss about things than my Aunt Gina!"

"Is your Aunt Gina bruised all over because you hit her?" Angelica demanded.

When they came to the half-open door at last, there was only another room, slightly smaller. This one had a carpet. Gilded sofas stood about like Dutch barns, and large frilly armchairs. Angelica gave a wail of despair.

Tonino stood on tiptoe. There seemed to be cushions on some of the seats. "Suppose we hid under a cushion for the night?" he suggested, trying to make peace.

Angelica turned on him furiously. "Stupid! No wonder you're slow at spells! We may be small, but they'll find us *because* of that. We must *stink* of magic. Even my baby brother could find us, and he may be a baby but he's cleverer than you!"

Tonino was too angry to answer. He simply marched away into the carpet. At first it was a relief to his sore feet, but it soon became another trial. It was like walking through long, tufty grass – and anyone who has done that for a mile or so will know how tiring that can be. On top of that, they had to keep going round puffy armchairs that seemed as big as houses, frilly footstools and screens as big as hoardings. Some of these things would have made good hiding-places, but they were both too angry and frightened to suggest it.

Then, when they reached the door at last, it was shut. They threw themselves against the hard wood. It did not even shake.

"Now what?" said Tonino, leaning his back against it. The moon was going down by now. The carpet was in darkness. The bars of moonlight from the far-off windows only touched the tops of armchairs, or picked out the gold on the sofa backs, or the glitter from a shelf of coloured glass vases. It would be quite dark soon.

"There's an Angel over there," Angelica said wearily.

She was right. Tonino could just see it, as coloured flickers on wood, lit by moonlight reflected off the shelf of glass vases. There was another door under the Angel, or rather a dark space, because that door was wide open. Too tired even to speak, Tonino set off again, across another mile of tufty carpet, past beetling cliffs of furniture, to the other side of the room.

By the time they reached that open door, they were so tired that nothing seemed real any more. There were four steps down beyond the door. Very well. They went down them somehow. At the bottom was an even more brutally tufted carpet. It was quite dark.

Angelica sniffed the darkness. "Cigars."

It could have been scillas for all Tonino cared. All he wanted was the next door. He set off, feeling round the walls for it, with Angelica stumbling after. They bumped into one huge piece of furniture, felt their way round it, and banged into another, which stuck even further into the room. And so they went, stumbling and banging, climbing across two rounded metal bars, wading in carpet, until they arrived at the four steps again. It was quite a small room – for the Palace – and it had only one door. Tonino felt for the first step, as high as his head, and did not think he had the strength to get up them again. The Angel had not been a guide after all.

"That part that stuck out," said Angelica. "I don't know what it was, but it was hollow, like a box. Shall we risk hiding in it?"

"Let's find it," said Tonino.

They found it, or something like it, by walking into it. It was a steep-sided box which came up to their armpits. There was a large piece of metal, like a very wide door-knocker, hung on the front of it. When they felt inside, they felt sheets of stiff leather, and crisper stuff that was possibly paper.

"I think it's an open drawer," said Tonino.

Angelica did not answer. She simply climbed in. Tonino heard her flapping and crackling among the paper – if it was paper. Well! he thought. And it was Angelica who said they smelt of magic. But he was so tired that he climbed in too, and fell into a warm crumply nest where Angelica was already asleep. Tonino was almost too tired by now to care if they were found or not. But he had the sense to drag a piece of parchment over them both before he went to sleep too.

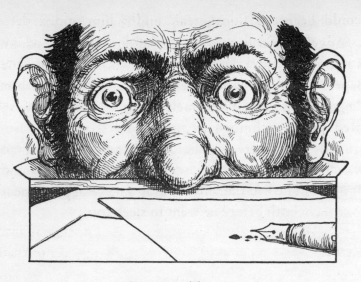

CHAPTER TWELVE

✳

*T*onino woke up feeling chilly and puzzled. The light was pale and yellow because his sheet seemed to be over his face. Tonino gazed up at it, thinking it was a surprisingly flat, stiff sheet. It had large black letters on it too. His eyes travelled along the letters. *DECLARATION OF WAR (Duplicate Copy)*, he read.

Then he knew, with a jump, that he was nine inches high and lying in a drawer in the Palace. And it was light! Someone would find them. In fact, someone nearly had. That was what had woken him. He could hear someone moving about the room, making obscure thumps and shuffles, and occasionally whistling a snatch of the *Angel of Caprona*.

Whoever it was had reached the drawer now. Tonino

could hear the floor creak under him and a dress rustling, loud and near. He moved his head, gently and stiffly, and found Angelica's frightened face resting on crumpled paper an inch or so away. The rustling dress proved the person was a woman. It must be the Duchess looking for them.

"That Duke!" said the person, in a voice no Duchess would use. "There never was such an untidy man!" Her breathing came suddenly nearer. Before either Tonino or Angelica could think what to do, the drawer moved. Helplessly, they were shunted inwards, feet first into darkness, and the drawer shut with a bang behind their heads.

"Help!" whispered Angelica.

"Ssh!"

The maid was still in the room. They could hear her move something, and then a tinkle of notes as she dusted a piano. Then a bump. And finally nothing. When they were quite sure she was gone, Angelica whispered, "What do we do now?"

There was room to sit up in the drawer, but not much else. Above their heads was a slit of light where the drawer met the desk, or whatever it was, and no way of opening it. But they could see quite well. Light was coming in at the back, beyond their feet. They tried bracing their hands against the wood overhead and heaving, but the drawer was made of solid, spicy-smelling wood and they could not budge it.

"We keep being shut in places without doors!" Angelica cried out. And she went floundering through the papers to the back of the drawer, where the light came in. Tonino crawled after her.

As soon as they got there, they realised this was the way out. The end of the drawer was lower than the front, and it did not reach the back of the wooden desk it was part of. There was quite a big gap there. When they put their heads into the space, they could see the ends of the other drawers above theirs going up like a ladder, and a slit of daylight at the top.

They squeezed through into the gap and climbed, side by side. It was as easy as climbing a ladder. They were one drawer away from the slit of daylight – which was going to be a tight squeeze – when they heard someone else in the room.

"They came down here, madam," said a lady's voice.

"Then we've caught them," replied the Duchess. "Look very carefully."

Tonino and Angelica hung from the back of the drawers by their fingers and toes, not daring to move. Silk dresses rustled as the Duchess and her lady moved round the room. "There's nothing this end at all, madam,"

"And I swear this window hasn't been opened," said the Duchess. "Open all the drawers in the desk."

There was a sharp rumble above Tonino's head. Dusty white light flooded down from the open top drawer. Papers were loudly tossed over. "Nothing," said the lady. The top drawer slammed in again. Tonino and Angelica had been hanging on to the second drawer. They climbed down to the next as fast and quietly as they could. The second drawer rumbled open, and slammed shut, nearly deafening them. The drawer they were on jerked. Luckily, it was stiff. The lady tugged and rattled at it, and that gave Tonino and Angelica just time to climb frantically up to the second drawer again and cling there. And there they hung, in the dark narrow space, while the lady opened the third drawer, slammed it shut, and pulled out the bottom drawer. They craned over their arms and watched the white light flood in from below.

"Look at this!" cried the lady. "They've been here! It's like a mouse-nest!"

Silks rustled as the Duchess hurried over. "Curse it!" she said. "Not long ago too! I can smell them even through the cigars. Quick! They can't be far away. They must have got out before the room was cleaned."

The drawer rumbled in, bringing dusty darkness with it. There was a flurry of silks as the two women hurried away up the steps to the room with the armchairs, and the quiet, firm *clap* of the door closing.

"Do you think it's a trap?" Angelica whispered.

"No," said Tonino. He was sure the Duchess had not guessed where they were. But they were shut in this room now, by the sound, and he had no idea how they would get the door open.

All the same, even a shut room was great open spaces compared with the narrow slit at the back of the drawers. Angelica and Tonino pushed and squeezed and forced themselves through the narrow daylight slit, and finally crawled out on the top of a writing-desk. Before their eyes had got used to the light, Tonino stubbed his toe on a vast pen like a telegraph pole and then tripped over a paper-knife like an ivory plank. Angelica bumped into a china ornament standing at the back of the desk. It swayed. She swayed. She flung her arms round it. When her eyes stopped watering, she found she was hugging a china Mr Punch, nose, red nightgown and all, about the same height as she was. There was a china Judy standing at the other end of the desk.

"We can't get away from these things!" she said.

The desk was covered in smooth red leather, very easy on the feet, and held a huge white blotter, which was even more comfortable to walk on. A chair with a matching red seat stood in front of the desk. Tonino saw they could easily jump down on to it. Even more easily, they could climb down the handles of the drawers. On the other hand, the piano the maid had dusted stood right beside the desk, and the window was round the corner from the piano. To reach the window was only a long stride from the piano. Though the window was shut, it had quite an easy-looking catch, if only they could reach it.

"Look!" said Angelica, pointing disgustedly.

A whole row of Punch and Judys stood along the top of the piano. Two were puppets on stands, very old and valuable by the look of them; two more were actually made of gold; and two others were rather arty clay models, which made Punch look like a leering ordinary man and Judy uncomfortably like the Duchess. And the music which was open on the piano was headed *Arnolfini – Punch and Judy Suite.*

"I think this is the Duke's study," said Angelica. And both of them got the giggles.

Still giggling, Tonino stepped on to the piano and started to walk to the window. *Do – ti – so – fa*, went the piano.

"Come back!" Angelica laughed.

Tonino came back – *fa – so – ti – do* – nearly in hysterics.

The door of the room opened and someone hurried down the steps. Angelica and Tonino could think of nothing better to do than stand stiffly where they were, hoping to be taken for more Punch and Judys. And, luckily, the man who came in was busy and worried. He slapped a pile of papers on the desk, without so much as glancing at the two new puppets, and hurried out again, gently closing the door behind him.

"Phew!" said Angelica.

They walked round to the front of the papers and looked at them curiously. The top one said:

Report of Campaign at 08.00 hours. Summary:
Troops advancing on all fronts to repel invasion.
Heavy Artillery and Reservists moving up in support.
Pisan front reports heavy losses. Fleet sighted –
Pisan? – steaming for mouth of Voltava.

"We're at war!" said Tonino. "Why?"

"Because the Duchess has got us, of course," said Angelica. "And our families daren't make war-spells. Tonino, we must get *out*. We must tell them where the words to the *Angel* are!"

"But why does the Duchess want Caprona beaten?" Tonino said.

"I don't know," said Angelica. "There's something wrong about her, I know that. Aunt Bella said there was an awful fuss when the Duke decided to marry her. Nobody likes her."

"Let's see if we can open the window," said Tonino. He set off along the piano again. **Do**-ti-so-*fa-me-re*—

"Quiet!" said Angelica.

Tonino discovered that, if he put each foot down very slowly, the notes did not sound. He was halfway along the keyboard, and Angelica had one foot stretched out to follow, when they heard someone opening the door again. There was no time to be careful. Angelica fled back to the desk. Tonino, with a terrible discord, scrambled across the black notes and squeezed behind the music on the stand.

He was only just in time. When he looked – he was standing with his feet and head sideways, like an Ancient Egyptian – the Duke of Caprona himself was standing in front of the desk. Tonino thought the Duke seemed both puzzled and sad. He was tapping the *Report of Campaign* against his teeth and did not seem to notice Angelica standing between the Punch and Judy on his desk, although Angelica's eyes were blinking against the glitter from the Duke's buttons.

"But I didn't declare war!" the Duke said to himself. "I was watching that puppet-show. How could I—?" He sighed and bit the *Report* worriedly between two rows of big shiny teeth. "Is my mind going?" he asked. He seemed to be talking to Angelica. She had the sense not to answer.

"I must go and ask Lucrezia," the Duke said. He

flung the *Report* down at Angelica's feet and hurried out of the study.

Tonino slid cautiously down the piano-lid on to the keys again – *ker-pling*. Angelica was now standing at the end of the piano, pointing at the window. She was speechless with horror.

Tonino looked – and for a moment he was as frightened as Angelica. There was a brown monster glaring at him through the glass, wide-faced, wide-eyed and shaggy. The thing had eyes like yellow lamps.

Faintly, through the glass, came a slightly irritable request to pull himself together and open the window.

"Benvenuto!" shouted Tonino.

"Oh – it's only a cat," Angelica quavered. "How terrible it must feel to be a mouse!"

"Just a cat!" Tonino said scornfully. "That's Benvenuto." He tried to explain to Benvenuto that it was not easy to open windows when you were nine inches high.

Benvenuto's impatient answer was to shove Tonino's latest magic exercise book in front of Tonino's mind's eye, open at almost the first page.

"Oh, thanks," Tonino said, rather ashamed. There were three opening-spells on that page, and none of them had stuck in his head. He chose the easiest, shut his eyes so that he could read the imaginary page more clearly, and sang the spell.

Gently and easily, the window swung open, letting in a gust of cold wind. And Benvenuto came in with the wind, almost as lightly. As Benvenuto trod gently up the scale towards him, Tonino had another moment when he knew how mice felt. Then he forgot it in the gladness of seeing Benvenuto. He stretched his arms wide to rub behind Benvenuto's horny ears.

Benvenuto put his sticky black nose to Tonino's face, and they both stood, delighted, holding down a long humming discord on the piano.

Benvenuto said that Paolo was not quick enough; he could not make him understand where Tonino was. Tonino must send Paolo a message. Could Tonino write this size?

"There's a pen on the desk here," Angelica called. And Tonino remembered her saying she could understand cats.

Rather anxiously, Benvenuto wanted to know if Tonino minded him talking to a Petrocchi.

The question astonished Tonino for a moment. He had clean forgotten that he and Angelica were supposed to hate one another. It seemed a waste of time, when they were both in such trouble. "Not at all," he said.

"Do get off that piano, both of you," said Angelica. "The humming's horrible."

Benvenuto obliged, with one great flowing leap. Tonino struggled after him with his elbows hooked over the piano-lid, pushing himself along against the black notes. By the time he reached the desk, Benvenuto and Angelica had exchanged formal introductions, and Benvenuto was advising them not to try getting out of the window. The room was three floors up. The stonework was crumbling, and even a cat had some trouble keeping his feet. If they would wait, Benvenuto would fetch help.

"But the Duchess—" said Tonino.

"And the Duke," said Angelica. "This is the Duke's study."

Benvenuto considered the Duke harmless on his own. He thought they were in the safest place in the Palace. They were to stay hidden and write him a note small enough to carry in his mouth.

"Wouldn't it be better if we tied it round your neck?" Angelica asked.

Benvenuto had never submitted to anything round his neck, and he was not going to start now. Anyway, someone in the Palace might see the message.

So Tonino put one foot on the *Report of Campaign* and succeeded, by heaving with both hands, in tearing off a corner of it. Angelica passed him the huge pen, which he had to hold in both hands, with the end resting on his shoulder. Then she stood on the paper to keep it steady while Tonino wielded the pen. It was such hard work, that he kept the message as short as possible. *In Duke's Palace. Duchess enchantress. T.M. & A.P.*

"Tell them about the words to the *Angel*," said Angelica. "Just in case."

Tonino turned the paper over and wrote *Words to* Angel *on Angel over gate. T & A.* Then, exhausted with heaving the pen up and down, he folded the piece of paper with that message inside and the first one outside, and trod it flat. Benvenuto opened his mouth. Angelica winced at that pink cavern with its arched wrinkly roof and its row of white fangs, and let Tonino place the message across Benvenuto's prickly tongue. Benvenuto gave Tonino a loving glare and sprang away. He struck one ringing chord from the piano, around middle C, made the slightest thump on the windowsill, and vanished.

Tonino and Angelica were staring after him and did not notice, until it was too late, that the Duke had come back.

"Funny," said the Duke. "There's a new Punch now, as well as a new Judy."

Tonino and Angelica stood stiff as posts, one on each end of the blotter, in agonisingly uncomfortable attitudes.

Fortunately, the Duke noticed the open window. "Blessed maids and their fresh air!" he grumbled, and went over to shut it. Tonino seized the opportunity to stand on both feet, Angelica to uncrick her neck. Then they both jumped. An unmistakable gunshot cracked out, from somewhere below. And another. The Duke bent out of the window and seemed to be watching something. "Poor pussy," he said. He sounded sad and resigned. "Why couldn't you keep away, puss? She hates cats. And they make such a din, too, shooting them." Another shot cracked out, and then several more. The Duke stood up, shaking his head sadly. "Ah well," he said, as he shut the window. "I suppose they do eat birds."

He came back across the study. Tonino and Angelica could not have moved if they tried. They were both too stricken.

The Duke's face folded into shiny wrinkles. He had noticed the corner torn from the *Report*. "I've been eating paper now!" he said. His sad, puzzled face turned towards Tonino and Angelica. "I think I do forget things," he said. "I talk to myself. That's a bad sign. But I really don't remember you two at all. At least, I remember the new

Judy, but," he said to Tonino, "I don't remember you at all. How did you get here?"

Tonino was far too upset about Benvenuto to think. After all, the Duke really was speaking to him. "Please, sir," he said, "I'll explain—"

"Shut *up*!" snapped Angelica. "I'll say a spell!"

"—only please tell me if they shot my cat," said Tonino.

"I think so," said the Duke. "It looked as if they got it." Here he took a deep breath and turned his eyes carefully to the ceiling, before he looked at Tonino and Angelica again. Neither of them moved. Angelica was glaring at Tonino, promising him spells unimaginable if he said another word. And Tonino knew he had been an utter idiot anyway. Benvenuto was dead and there was no point in moving – no point in anything.

The Duke, meanwhile, slowly pulled a large handkerchief out of his pocket. A slightly crumpled cigar came out with it and flopped on the desk. The Duke picked it up and put it absent-mindedly between his glistening teeth. And then he had to take it out again to wipe his shiny face. "Both of you spoke," he said, putting the handkerchief away and fetching out a gold lighter. "You know that?" he said, putting the cigar back into his mouth. He gave a furtive look round, clicked the lighter, and lit the cigar. "You are looking," he said, "at a poor dotty Duke." Smoke rolled out with his words, as much smoke as if the Duke had been a dragon.

Angelica sneezed. Tonino thought he was going to sneeze. He drew a deep breath to stop himself and burst out coughing.

"Ahah!" cried the Duke. "Got you!" His large wet hands pounced, and seized each of them round the legs. Holding them like that, firmly pinned to the blotter, he sat down in the chair and bent his triumphant shiny face until it was level with theirs. The cigar, cocked out of one side of his mouth, continued to roll smoke over them. They flailed their arms for balance and coughed and coughed. "Now what are you?" said the Duke. "Another of her fiendish devices for making me think I'm potty? Eh?"

"No we're not!" coughed Tonino, and Angelica coughed, "Oh, please stop that smoke!"

The Duke laughed. "The old Chinese cigar-torture," he said gleefully, "guaranteed to bring statues to life." But his right hand moved Tonino, stumbling and swaying, across the blotter to Angelica, where his left hand gathered him in. His right hand took the cigar out of his mouth and laid it on the edge of the desk. "Now," he said. "Let's have a look at you."

They scrubbed their streaming eyes and looked fearfully up at his great grinning face. It was impossible to look at all of it at once. Angelica settled for his left eye, Tonino for his right eye. Both eyes bulged at them, round and innocent, like Old Niccolo's.

"Bless me!" said the Duke. "You're the spell-makers' children who were supposed to come to my pantomime! Why didn't you come?"

"We never got an invitation, Your Grace," Angelica said. "Did you?" she asked Tonino.

"No," Tonino said mournfully.

The Duke's face sagged. "So that's why it was. I wrote

them myself too. That's my life in a nutshell. None of the orders I give ever get carried out, and an awful lot of things get done that I never ordered at all." He opened his hand slowly. The big warm fingers peeled damply off their legs. "You feel funny wriggling about in my hand," he said. "There, if I let you go, will you tell me how you got here?"

They told him, with one or two forced pauses when he took a puff at his cigar and set them coughing again. He listened wonderingly. It was not like explaining things to a huge grown-up Duke. Tonino felt as if he was telling a made-up story to his small cousins. From the way the Duke's eyes popped, and the way he kept saying "Go on!" Tonino was sure the Duke was believing it no more than the little Montanas believed the story of Giovanni the Giant Killer.

Yet, when they had finished, the Duke said, "That Punch and Judy show started at eight-thirty and went on till nine-fifteen. I know, because there was a clock just over you. They say I declared war at nine o'clock last night. Did either of you notice me declaring war?"

"No," they said. "Though," Angelica added sourly, "I was being beaten to death at the time and I might not have noticed."

"My apologies," said the Duke. "But did either of you hear gunfire? No. But firing started around eleven and went on all night. It's still going on. You can see it, but not hear it, from the tower over this study. Which means another damn spell, I suppose. And I think I'm supposed to sit here and not notice Caprona being blown to pieces around me." He put his chin in his hands and stared at them miserably. "I know I'm a fool," he said, "but just because I love plays and puppet-theatres, I'm not an idiot. The question is, how do we get you two out of here without Lucrezia knowing?"

Tonino and Angelica were almost too surprised and grateful to speak. And while they were still trying to say thank you, the Duke jumped upright, staring pop-eyed.

"She's coming! I've got an instinct. Quick! Get in my pockets!"

He turned round sideways to the desk and held one pocket of his coat stretched against it, between two fingers. Angelica hastily lifted the pocket-flap and slid down between the two layers of cloth. The Duke stubbed out his cigar on the edge of the desk and popped it in after her. Then he turned round and held the other pocket open for Tonino. As Tonino crouched down in fuzzy darkness, he heard the door open and the voice of the Duchess.

"My lord, you've been smoking cigars in here again."

CHAPTER THIRTEEN

✳

*P*aolo woke up that morning knowing that he was going to have to look for Tonino himself. If his father, and Rinaldo, and then Rosa and Marco, all refused to try, then there was no use asking anyone else.

He sat up and realised that the Casa was full of unusual noises. Below in the yard, the gate was open. He could hear the voices of Elizabeth, Aunt Anna, Aunt Maria and Cousin Claudia, who were bringing the day's bread.

"Just look at the Angel!" he heard his mother say. "Now what did that?"

"It's because we've stopped our spells," said Cousin Claudia.

Following that came a single note of song from Aunt Anna, cut off short with a squeak.

Aunt Maria said angrily, "No spells, Anna! Think of Tonino!"

This was intriguing, but what really interested Paolo were the noises behind the voices: marching feet, orders being shouted, a drum beating, horses' hooves, heavy rumbling and some cursing. Paolo shot out of bed. It must be the army.

"Hundreds of them," he heard Aunt Anna say.

"Most of them younger than my Domenico," said Aunt Maria. "Claudia, take this basket while I shut the gate. All going to face three armies without a war-scrip between them. I could cry!"

Paolo shot along the gallery, pulling on his jacket, and hurried down the steps into the cold yellow sunlight. He was too late. The gate was barred and the war-noises shut out. The ladies were crossing the yard with their baskets.

"Where do you think you're going?" Elizabeth called to him. "No one's going out today. There's going to be fighting. The schools are all closed."

They put down their baskets to open the kitchen door. Paolo saw them recoil, with cries of dismay.

"Good Lord!" said Elizabeth.

"Don't anyone tell Gina!" said Aunt Maria.

At the same moment, someone knocked heavily at the Casa gate.

"See who that is, Paolo," called Aunt Anna.

Paolo went under the archway and undid the flap of the peephole. He was pleased to have this chance to see the army, and pleased that the schools were shut. He had not intended to go to school today anyway.

There was a man in uniform outside, who shouted, "Open and receive this, in the name of the Duke!" Behind him, Paolo caught glimpses of shiny marching boots and more uniforms. He unbarred the gate.

Meanwhile, it became plain that Aunt Gina was not to be kept away from the kitchen. Her feet clattered on the stairs. There was a stunned pause. Then the whole Casa filled with her voice.

"Oh my God! Mother of God! *Insects!*" It even drowned the noise of the military band that was marching past as Paolo opened the gate.

The man outside thrust a sheet of paper at Paolo and darted off to hammer on the next door. Paolo looked at it. He had a mad idea that he had just been handed the words to the *Angel*. After that, he went on staring, oblivious alike of Aunt Gina – who was now screaming what she was going to do to Lucia – and of the great gun that went rumbling past, pulled by four straining horses.

State of Caprona, Paolo read, *Form FR3 Call Up of Final Reservists. The following to report to the Arsenal for immediate duty at 03.00 hrs, January 14th, 1979: Antonio Montana, Lorenzo Montana, Piero Montana, Ricardo Montana, Arturo Montana (ne Notti), Carlo Montana, Luigi Montana, Angelo Montana, Luca Montana, Giovanni Montana, Piero Iacopo Montana, Rinaldo Montana, Domenico Montana, Francesco Montana.*

That was everyone! Paolo had not realised that even his father was a Final Reservist.

"Shut the gate, Paolo!" shrieked Aunt Maria.

Paolo was about to obey, when he remembered that he had not yet looked at the Angel. He dodged outside and stared up, while half a regiment of infantry marched past behind him. It looked as if, in the night, every pigeon in Caprona had chosen to sit on that one golden carving. It was plastered with bird-droppings. They were particularly thick, not unnaturally, on the outstretched arm holding the scroll, and the scroll was a crusty white mass. Paolo shuddered. It seemed like an omen. He did not notice one of the marching soldiers detach himself from the column and come up behind him.

"I should close the gate, if I were you," said Chrestomanci.

Paolo looked up at him and wondered why people looked so different in uniform. He pulled himself together and dragged the two halves of the gate shut. Chrestomanci helped him slot the big iron bars in to lock it. As he did, he said, "I was at the Casa Petrocchi around dawn, so there's no great need for explanations. But I would like to know what's the matter in the kitchen this time."

Paolo looked. Eight baskets piled high with round tan-coloured loaves stood outside the kitchen. There were agitated noises from inside it, and a curious long droning-sound. "I think it's Lucia's spell again," he said.

He and Chrestomanci set off across the yard. Before they had gone three steps, the aunts burst out of the kitchen and rushed towards him. Antonio and the uncles hurried down from the gallery, and cousins arrived from everywhere else.

Aunt Francesca surged out of the Saloon. She had spent the night there, and looked as if she had. Chrestomanci was soon in the middle of a crowd and holding several conversations at once.

"You were quite right to call me," he said to Rosa, and to Aunt Francesca, "Old Niccolo is good for years yet, but you should rest." To Elizabeth and Antonio, he said, "I know about Tonino," and to Rinaldo, "This is my fourth uniform today. There's heavy fighting in the hills and I had to get through somehow. What possessed the Duke," he asked the uncles, "to declare war so soon? I could have got help from Rome if he'd waited." None of them knew, and they all told him so at once. "I know," said Chrestomanci. "I know. No war-spells. I think our enemy enchanter has made a mistake over Tonino and Angelica. If it does nothing else, it allows me a free hand." Then, as the clamour showed no sign of abating, he said, "By the way, the Final Reserve has been called up," and nodded to Paolo to give the paper to Antonio.

In the sober hush that this produced, Chrestomanci pushed his way to the kitchen and put his head inside. "My goodness me!" Paolo heard him murmur.

Paolo ducked under all the people crowding round Antonio and looked into the kitchen under Chrestomanci's elbow. He looked into a wall of insects. The place was black with them, and glittering, and crawling, and dense with different humming. Flies of all kinds, mosquitoes, wasps and midges filled the air-space. Beetles, ants, moths and a hundred other crawling things occupied the floor and shelves and sink.

Peering through the buzzing clouds, Paolo was almost sure he saw a swarm of locusts on the cooking-stove. It was even worse than he had imagined the Petrocchi kitchen when he was little.

Chrestomanci drew a deep breath. Paolo suspected he was trying not to laugh. They both looked round for Lucia, who was standing on one leg among the breadbaskets, wondering whether to run away. "I am sure," Chrestomanci said to her – he *was* trying not to laugh; he had to start again. "I am sure people have talked to you about misusing spells. But – just out of interest – what did you use?"

"She used her own words to the *Angel of Caprona*!" Aunt Maria said, bursting angrily out of the crowd. "Gina's nearly out of her mind!"

"All the children did it," Lucia said defiantly. "It wasn't only me."

Chrestomanci looked at Paolo, and Paolo nodded. "A considerable tribute to the powers of the younger Montanas," said Chrestomanci. He turned and snapped his fingers into the buzzing, crawling kitchen. Not much happened. The air cleared enough for Paolo to see that it was indeed locusts on the cooker, but that was all. Chrestomanci's eyebrows went up a little. He tried again. This time nothing happened at all. He retreated from the buzzing, looking thoughtful.

"With all due respect," he said to Paolo and Lucia, "to the *Angel of Caprona*, it should not be this powerful on its own. I'm afraid this spell will just have to wear itself out." And he said to Aunt Maria, "No wonder the enemy enchanter is so much afraid of the Casa Montana. Does this mean there won't be any breakfast?"

"No, no. We'll make it in the dining-room," Aunt Maria said, looking very flustered.

"Good," said Chrestomanci. "There's something I have to say to everyone, when they're all there."

And when everyone was gathered round the tables to eat plain rolls and drink black coffee made over the dining-room fire, Chrestomanci stood in front of the fire, holding a coffee cup, and said, "I know few of you believe Tonino is not in the Casa Petrocchi, but I swear to you he is not, and that Angelica Petrocchi is also missing. I think you are quite right to stop making spells until they are found, but I want to say this: even if I found Tonino and Angelica this minute, all the spells of the Casa Montana and the Casa Petrocchi are not going to save Caprona now. There are three armies, and the fleet of Pisa, closing in on her. The *only thing* which is going to help you is the true words to the *Angel of Caprona*. Have you all understood?"

They all had. Everyone was silent. Nobody spoke for some time. Then Uncle Lorenzo began grumbling. Moths had got into his Reservist uniform. "Someone took the spell out," he complained. "I shan't be fit to be seen."

"Does it matter?" asked Rinaldo. His face was very white and he was not having anything but coffee. "You'll only be seen dead anyway."

"But that's just it!" said Uncle Lorenzo. "I don't want to be seen dead in it!"

"Oh be quiet!" Domenico snapped at him. Uncle Lorenzo was so surprised that he stopped talking. Breakfast finished in gloomy murmurs.

Paolo got up and slid behind the bench where

Chrestomanci was sitting. "Excuse me, sir. Do you know where Tonino is?"

"I wish I did," said Chrestomanci. "This enchanter is good. So far, I have only two clues. Last night, when I was coming up through Siena, somebody worked two very strange spells somewhere ahead of me."

"Tonino?" Paolo said eagerly.

Chrestomanci shook his head. "The first one was definitely Angelica. She has what you might call an individual style. But the other one baffled me. Do you think your brother is capable of working anything strong enough to get through an enchanter's spells? Angelica did it through sheer weirdness. Could Tonino, do you think?"

"I shouldn't think so," said Paolo. "He doesn't know many spells, but he always gets them right and they work—"

"Then it remains a mystery," said Chrestomanci. He sighed. Paolo thought he looked tired.

"Thanks," he said, and slipped off, carefully thinking careless thoughts about what he would do now school was closed. He did not want anyone to notice what he meant to do.

He slipped through the coach-house, past the crumpled horses and coachman, past the coach, and opened the little door in the wall at the back. He was half through it, when Rosa said doubtfully, at the front of the coach-house, "Paolo? Are you in there?"

No, I'm not, Paolo thought, and shut the little door after him as gently as he knew how. Then he ran.

By this time, there were hardly any soldiers in the

streets, and hardly anyone else either. Paolo ran past yellow houses, heavily shuttered, in a quiet broken by the uneasy ringing of bells. From time to time, he thought he could hear a dull, distant noise – a sort of booming, with a clatter in its midst. Wherever the houses opened out and Paolo could see the hills, he saw soldiers – not as soldiers, but as crawling, twinkling lines, winding upwards – and some puffs of smoke. He knew Chrestomanci was right. The fighting was very near.

He was the only person about in the Via Cantello. The Casa Petrocchi was as shuttered and barred as the Casa Montana. And their Angel was covered with bird-lime too. Like the Montanas, they had stopped making spells. Which showed, thought Paolo, that Chrestomanci was right about Angelica too. He was much encouraged by that as he hammered on the rough old gate.

There was no sound from inside, but, after a second or so, a white cat jumped to the top of the gate, and crouched in the gap under the archway, looking down with eyes even bluer than Paolo's.

Those eyes reminded Paolo that his own eyes were likely to give him away. He did not think he dared disguise them with a spell, in case the Petrocchis noticed. So he swallowed, told himself that he had to find the one person who was likely to help him look for Tonino, and said to the cat, "Renata. Could I speak to Renata?"

The white cat stared. Maybe it made some remark. Then it jumped down inside the Casa, leaving Paolo with an uncomfortable feeling that it knew who he was. But he waited. Before he had quite decided to go away again, the peephole was unlatched. To his relief, it was Renata's pointed face that looked through the bars at him.

"Whoops!" she said. "I see why Vittoria fetched *me*. What a relief you came!"

"Come and help find Tonino and Angelica," said Paolo. "Nobody will listen."

"Ung." Renata pulled a strip of her red hair into her mouth and bit it. "We're forbidden to go out. Think of an excuse."

"Your teacher's ill and scared of the war and wants us to sit with her," said Paolo.

"That might do," said Renata. "Come in while I ask." Paolo heard the gate being unbarred. "Her name's Mrs Grimaldi," Renata whispered, holding the gate open for him. "She lives in the Via Sant' Angelo and she's ever so ugly, in case they ask. Come in."

Considerably to his amazement, Paolo entered the Casa Petrocchi, and was even more amazed not to be particularly frightened. He felt as if he was about to do an exam, keyed up, and knowing he was in for it, but that was all.

He saw a yard and a gallery so like his own that he could almost have believed he had been magically whisked back home. There were differences, of course. The gallery railings were fancy wrought-iron, with iron leopards in them at intervals. The cats that sat sunning themselves on the water butts were mostly ginger or tabby – whereas in the Casa Montana, Benvenuto had left his mark, and the cats were either black or black and white. And there was a gush of smell from the kitchen – frying onions – the like of which Paolo had not smelt since Lucia cast her unlucky spell.

"Mother!" shouted Renata.

But the first person who appeared was Marco. Marco was galloping down the steps from the gallery with a pair of long shiny boots in one hand, and a crumpled red uniform over his arm. "Mother!" Marco bellowed, in the free and easy way people always bellow for their mothers. "Mother! There's moth in my uniform! Who took the spell out of it?"

"Stupid!" Renata said to him. "We put every single spell away last night." And she said to Paolo, "That's my brother Marco."

Marco turned indignantly to Renata. "But moths take months—!" And he saw Paolo. It was hard to tell which of them was more dismayed.

At that moment, a red-haired, worried-looking lady came across the yard, carrying a little boy. The baby had black hair and the same bulging forehead as Angelica. "I don't know, Marco," she said. "Get Rosa to mend it. What is it, Renata?"

Marco interrupted. "Rosa," he said, looking fixedly at Paolo, "is with her *sister*. Who's your friend, Renata?"

Paolo could not resist. "I'm Paolo Andretti," he said wickedly. Marco rewarded him with a look which dared him to say another word.

Renata was relieved, because she now knew what to call Paolo. "Paolo wants me to come and help look after Mrs Grimaldi. She's ill in bed, Mother."

Paolo could see by the way Marco's eyes went first

wide and then almost to slits, that Marco was extremely alarmed by this and determined to stop Renata. But Paolo could not see how Marco could do anything. He could not give away that he knew who Paolo was without giving away himself and Rosa too. It made him want to laugh.

"Oh poor Mrs Grimaldi!" said Mrs Petrocchi. "But, Renata, I don't think—"

"Doesn't Mrs Grimaldi realise there's a war on?" Marco said. "Did Paolo tell you she was ill?"

"Yes," Paolo said glibly. "My mother's great friends with Mrs Grimaldi. She's sorry for her because she's so ugly."

"And of course she knows about the war." Renata said. "I kept telling you, Marco, how she dives under her desk if she hears a bang. She's scared stiff of guns."

"And it's all been too much for her, Mother says," Paolo added artistically.

Marco tried another tack. "But why does Mrs Grimaldi want *you*, Renata? Since when have you been teacher's pet?"

Renata, who was obviously as quick as Paolo, said, "Oh, I'm not. She just wants me to amuse her with some spells—"

At this, Mrs Petrocchi and Marco said, "You're not to use spells! Angelica—"

"—but of course I won't," Renata continued smoothly. "I'll just sing songs. She likes me to sing. And Paolo's going to read to her out of the Bible. Do say we can go, Mother. She's lying in bed all on her own."

"Well—" said Mrs Petrocchi.

"The streets aren't safe," said Marco.

"There was no one about at all," Paolo said, giving Marco a look to make him watch it. Two could play at that.

"Mother," said Renata, "you *are* going to mend Marco's uniform, aren't you?"

"Yes, yes, of course," said Mrs Petrocchi.

Renata at once took this as permission to go with Paolo. "Come on, Paolo," she said, and raced under Marco's nose to what was obviously the coach-house. Paolo whizzed after her.

Marco, however, was not defeated. Before Renata's hand was on the latch of the big door, an obvious uncle was leaning over the gallery. "Renata! Be a good girl and find me my tobacco." An obvious aunt shot out of the kitchen. She looked like Aunt Gina with red hair, and she hooted in the same way. "Renata! Have you taken my good knife?" Two young cousins shot out of another door. "Renata, you said you'd play dressing-up!" and Mrs Petrocchi, looking anxious and undecided, was holding the baby boy out, saying, "Renata, you'll have to mind Roberto while I'm sewing."

"I can't stop now!" Renata shouted back. "Poor Mrs Grimaldi!" She wrenched open the big door and pushed Paolo inside. "What's going on?" she whispered.

It was obvious to Paolo what was going on. It was so like the Casa Montana. Marco had broadcast – not an alarm, because he dared not – a sort of general uneasiness about Renata. "Marco's trying to stop us," he said.

"I know *that*," Renata said, hurrying him past the sleek

Petrocchi coach and – to Paolo's interest – past four black cardboard horses as crumpled and muddy as the Casa Montana ones. "*Why* is he? How does he know?"

Behind them was a perfect clamour of Petrocchi voices, all wanting Renata. "He just does," Paolo said. "Be quick!"

The small door to the street had a big stiff key. Renata took it in both hands and struggled to turn it. "Does he know *you*?" she said sharply.

Like an answer, Marco's voice sounded from behind the coach. "Renata!" Then, much more softly, "Paolo – Paolo Montana, come here!"

The door came open. "Run, if you're coming!" Paolo said. They shot out into the street, both running hard. Marco came to the door and shouted something, but he did not seem to be following. Nevertheless, Paolo kept on running, which forced Renata to run too. He did not want to talk. He wanted to absorb the shock of Marco. Marco Andretti was really Marco Petrocchi – he must be Guido's eldest son! Rosa Montana and Marco Petrocchi. How did they do it? How ever did they *manage* it? he kept wondering. And also – more soberly – How ever will they get away with it?

"All right. That will do," Renata panted. By this time they had crossed the Corso and were down beside the river, trotting along empty quaysides towards the New Bridge. Renata slowed down, and Paolo did too, quite breathless. "Now," she said, "tell me how Marco knew you, or I won't come a step further."

Paolo looked at her warily. He had already discovered

that Renata was, as Aunt Gina would say, sharp enough to cut herself, and he did not like the way she was looking at him. "He saw me at the Palace of course," Paolo said.

"No he didn't," said Renata. "He drove the coach. He knows your name *and* he knows why you came, doesn't he? How?"

"I think he must have been standing behind us on the Art Gallery steps, and we didn't see him in the fog," said Paolo.

Renata's shrewd eyes continued the look Paolo did not like.

"Good try," she said. Paolo tried to break off the look by turning and sauntering on along the quays. Renata followed him, saying, "And I was meant to get all embarrassed and not ask any more. You're sharp enough to cut yourself, Mr Montana. But what a pity. Marco wasn't in the fight. They wanted him for the single combat, that's how I know, and he wasn't there, so Papa had to do it. And I can tell that you don't want me to know how Marco knows you. And I can tell Marco doesn't, or he'd have stopped me going by saying who you were. So—"

"You're the one who's going to cut yourself," Paolo said over his shoulder, "by being too clever. I don't know how Marco knew me, but he was being kind not say—" He stopped. He sniffed. He was level with an alleyway, where a peeling blue house bulged out on to the jetty. Paolo felt the air round that alley with a sense he hardly knew he had, inborn over generations of spellmaking. A spell had been set here – a strong spell, not long ago.

Renata came up behind. "You're not going to wriggle out—" She stopped too. "Someone made a spell here!"

"Was it Angelica? Can you tell?" Paolo asked.

"Why?" said Renata.

Paolo told her what Chrestomanci had said. Her face went red, and she prodded with her toe at a mooring-chain in the path. "Individual style!" she said. "Him and his jokes! It's not Angelica's fault. She was born that way. And it's not everyone who can get a spell to work by doing everything wrong. I think she's a sort of back-to-front genius, and I told the Duchess of Caprona so when she laughed, too!"

"But is the spell hers?" asked Paolo. He could hear gunfire, from somewhere down the river, mixed with the dull booming from the hills. It was a blunt, bonking *clomp, clomp*, like a giant chopping wood. His head went up to listen as he said, "I know it's not Tonino. His feel careful."

"No," said Renata, and her head was up too. "It's a bit stale, isn't it? And it doesn't feel very nice. The war sounds awfully close. I think we ought to get off the quays."

She was probably right. Paolo hesitated. He was sure they were hot on the trail. The stale spell had a slight sick feeling to it, which reminded him of the message in the yard last night.

And while he hesitated, the war seemed suddenly right on top of them. It was deafening, brazen, horrible. Paolo thought of someone holding one end of an acre of sheet metal and flapping it, or of gigantic alarm clocks. But that did not do justice to the noise. Nor did it account for some huge metallic screeches. He and

Renata ducked and put their hands to their ears, and enormous things whirled above them. They went on, whatever they were, out above the river. Paolo and Renata crouched on the quay, staring at them.

They flapped across in a group – there were at least eight of them – gonging and screeching. Paolo thought first of flying machines and then of the Montana winged horse. There seemed to be legs dangling beneath the great black bodies, and their metal wings were whirling furiously. Some of them were not flying so well. One lost height, despite madly clanging with its wings, and dropped into the river with a splash that threw water all over the New Bridge and spattered Renata and Paolo. Another one lost height and whirled its iron tail for balance. Paolo recognised it as one of the iron griffins from the Piazza Nuova, as it, too, fell into a spout of water.

Renata began to laugh. "Now that *is* Angelica!" she said. "I'd know her spells anywhere."

They leapt up and raced for the long flight of stairs up to the Piazza Nuova. The din from the griffins was still drowning all but the nearest gunfire. Renata and Paolo ran up the steps, turning round at every landing to see what was happening to the rest of the griffins. Two more came down in the river. A further two plunged into the gardens of rich villas. But the last two were going well. When Paolo next looked, they seemed to be struggling to gain altitude in order to get over the hills beyond the Palace. The distant clanging was fast and furious, and the metal wings a blur.

Paolo and Renata turned and climbed again.

"What is it? A call for help?" panted Paolo.

"Must be," gasped Renata. "Angelica's spells – always – mad kind of reasonableness."

An echoing clang brought them whirling round. Another griffin was down, but they did not see where. Fascinated, they watched the efforts of the last one. It had now reached the marble front of the Duke's Palace, and it was not high enough to clear it. The griffin seemed to know. It put out its claws and seemed to be clutching at the zig-zag marble battlements. But that did no good. They saw it, a distant black blot, go sliding down the coloured marble facade – they could even hear the grinding – down and down, until it crashed on to the roof of the marble gateway, where it drooped and lay still. Above it, even from here, they could see two long lines of scratches, all down the front of the Palace.

"Wow!" said Paolo.

He and Renata climbed up into the strangely bare Piazza Nuova. It was now nothing but a big paved platform surrounded by a low wall. At intervals round the wall were the snapped-off stumps of the griffins' pedestals, each with a broken green or crimson plaque lying beside it. In the middle, what had been a tangled griffin-fountain was now a jet of water from a broken pipe.

"Just look at all these spells she's broken!" exclaimed Renata. "I didn't think she could do anything this strong!"

Paolo looked across at the scratched Palace, rather enviously. There were spells in the marble to stop that kind of thing. Angelica must have broken them all. The odd thing was that he could not feel the spell. The Piazza

Nuova ought to have reeked of magic, but it just felt empty. He stared round, puzzled. And there, trotting slowly and wearily along the low wall, was a familiar brown shape with a trailing bush of a tail.

"Benvenuto!" he said.

For a moment, it looked as if Benvenuto was going to walk straight past Paolo, as he so often did. But that must have been because he was tired. He stopped. He glared urgently at Paolo. Then he carefully opened his mouth and spat out a small folded scrap of paper. After that, he lay down and lost interest in the world. Paolo could see his brown sides heaving when he picked up the paper.

Renata looked over Paolo's shoulder as Paolo – rather disgustedly, because it was wet – unfolded the paper. The writing was definitely Tonino's, though it was far too small. And, though Paolo did not know it, not much of Tonino's message had survived. He and Renata read:

ords to Angel on Angel over

It was small wonder that Paolo and Renata misunderstood. From the Piazza Nuova, now the griffins were gone, an Angel was clearly visible. It stood, golden and serene, guarding a Caprona which was already surrounded in the smoke from gunfire, on top of the great dome of the Cathedral.

"Do you think we can get up there?" said Paolo.

Renata's face was white. "We'd better try. But I warn you, I'm no good at heights."

They hurried down among the red roofs and golden

walls, leaving Benvenuto asleep on the wall. After a while, Benvenuto picked himself up and trotted away, restored. It took more than a few ill-aimed rifles to finish Benvenuto.

When Paolo and Renata reached the cobbled square in front of the Cathedral, the great bell in the bell-tower beside it was tolling. People were gathering into the church to pray for Caprona, and the Archbishop of Caprona himself was standing by the door blessing everyone who entered. Renata and Paolo joined the line. It seemed the easiest way to get in. They had nearly reached the door, when Marco dashed into the square towing Rosa. Rosa saw Renata's hair and pointed. She was too blown to speak. Marco grinned. "Your spell wins," he said.

CHAPTER FOURTEEN

✳

The warm pocket holding Tonino swayed and swooped as the Duke stood up. "Of course I smoked a cigar," he said to the Duchess, injured. "Anyone would smoke a cigar, if they found they'd declared war without knowing they had, and knew they were bound to be beaten." His voice came rumbling to Tonino's ears through his body, more than from outside.

"I've told you it's bad for your health," said the Duchess. "Where are you going?"

"Me? Oh," said the Duke. The pockets swooped, then swooped again, as he climbed the steps to the door. "Off to the kitchens. I feel peckish."

"You could send for food," said the Duchess, but she did not sound displeased. Tonino knew she had guessed they had been in the study all along and wanted the Duke out of it while she found them.

He heard the door shut. The pocket swung rhythmically as the Duke walked. It was not too bad once Tonino was used to it. It was a large pocket. There was almost room in it for Tonino, and the Duke's lighter, and his handkerchief, and another cigar, and some string, and some money, and a rosary, and some dice. Tonino made himself comfortable with the handkerchief as a cushion and wished the Duke would not keep patting at him to see if he was there.

"Are you all right in there?" the Duke rumbled at last. "Nobody about. You can stick your heads out. I thought of the kitchens because you didn't seem to have had any breakfast."

"You are kind," Angelica's voice came faintly. Tonino worked himself to his feet and put his head out under the flap of the pocket. He still could not see Angelica – the Duke's generous middle was in the way – but he heard her say, "You keep rather a lot of things in your pockets, don't you? Do you happen to know what I've got stuck to my foot?"

"Er – toffee, I suspect," said the Duke. "Please oblige me by eating it."

"Thanks," Angelica said doubtfully.

"I say," said Tonino. "Why didn't the Duchess know we were in your pockets? She could smell us before."

The Duke's loud laugh rumbled through him. The gilded wall Tonino could see began to jolt upward, and upward, and upward. The Duke was walking downstairs.

"Cigars, lad!" the Duke said. "Why do you think I smoke them? She can't smell anything through them, and she hates that. She tried setting a spell on me to make me stop once, but I got so bad-tempered she had to take it off."

"Excuse me, sir," came Angelica's voice from the other side of the Duke. "Won't someone notice if you walk downstairs talking to yourself?"

The Duke laughed again. "Not a soul! I talk to myself all the time – and laugh, too, if something amuses me. They all think I'm potty anyway. Now, have you two thought of a way to get you out of here? The safest way would be to fetch your families here. Then I could hand you over in secret, and she'd be none the wiser."

"Can't you just send for them?" Tonino suggested. "Say you need them to help in the war."

"She'd smell a rat," said the Duke. "She says your war-charms are all washed-up anyway. Think of something that's nothing to do with the war."

"Special effects for another pantomime," Tonino suggested, rather hopelessly. But he could see that even the Duke was not likely to produce a play while Caprona was being invaded.

"I know," said Angelica. "I shall cast a spell."

"No!" said Tonino. "Anything might happen!"

"That doesn't matter," said Angelica. "My family would know it's me, and they'd come here like a shot."

"But you might turn the Duke green!" said Tonino.

"I really wouldn't mind," the Duke put in mildly.

He came to the bottom of the stairs and went with long, charging strides through rooms and corridors of the

Palace. Angelica and Tonino each held on to an edge of their pockets and shouted arguments round him.

"But you could help me," said Angelica, "and your part would go right. Suppose we made it a calling-charm to fetch all the rats and mice in Caprona to the Palace. If you did the calling, we'd fetch something."

"Yes, but what would it be?" said Tonino.

"We could make it in honour of Benvenuto," shouted Angelica, hoping to please him.

But Tonino thought of Benvenuto lying somewhere on a Palace roof and became more obstinate than ever. He shouted that he was not going to do anything so disrespectful.

"Are you telling me you can't do a calling-spell?" shrieked Angelica. "Even my baby brother—"

They were shouting so loudly that the Duke had to tell them to shush twice. The military man hurrying up to the Duke stared slightly. "No need to stare, Major," the Duke said to him. "I said Shush and I meant Shush. Your boots squeak. What is it?"

"I'm afraid the forces of Caprona are in retreat in the south, Your Grace," said the soldier. "And our coastal batteries have fallen to the Pisan fleet."

Both pockets drooped as the Duke's shoulders slumped. "Thank you," he said. "Report to me personally next time you have news." The Major saluted and went, glancing at the Duke once or twice over his shoulder. The Duke sighed. "There goes another one who thinks I'm mad. Didn't you two say you were the only ones who knew where to find the words to the *Angel*?"

Tonino and Angelica put their heads out of his pockets again. "Yes," they said.

"Then," said the Duke, "will you please agree on a spell. You really must get out and get those words while there's still some of Caprona left."

"All right," said Tonino. "Let's call mice." He had not seen it was so urgent.

So the Duke stood in a wide window-bay and lit the cigar stub from under Angelica with the lighter from under Tonino, to cover up the spell. Tonino leant out of his pocket and sang, slowly and carefully, the only calling-spell he knew.

Angelica stood in the other pocket with her arms upraised and spoke, quickly, confidently and – quite certainly – wrong. Afterwards, she swore it was because she nearly laughed.

Another man approached. Tonino thought it was one of the courtiers who had watched the puppet show, but he was never sure, because the Duke flipped his pocket-flaps down over their heads and began singing himself.

"Merrily his music ringing,
See an Angel cometh singing..."

roared the Duke. Even Angelica did not sing so much out of tune. Tonino had the greatest difficulty in keeping up his own song. And it was certainly around then that the spell seemed to go wrong. Tonino had the sudden feeling that his words were pulling a great weight.

The Duke broke off his abominable singing to say,

"Ah, Pollio, there's nothing like a good song while Caprona burns! Nero did it, and now me."

"Yes, Your Grace," the man said feebly. They heard him scuttle away.

"And he's *sure* I'm mad," said the Duke. "Finished?"

Just then, Tonino's words came loose, with a sort of jerk, and he knew the spell had worked in some way or another. "Yes," he said.

But nothing seemed to happen. The Duke philosophically that it would take a mouse quite a while to run from the Corso to the Palace, and strode on to the kitchens. They thought he was mad there, too, Tonino could tell. The Duke asked for two bread rolls and two pats of butter and solemnly put one into each pocket. No doubt they thought he was madder still when he remarked to no one: "There's a cigar cutter in my right pocket that spreads butter quite well."

"Indeed, Your Grace?" they heard someone say dubiously.

Just then, someone rushed in screaming about the griffins from the Piazza Nuova. They were flying across the river, straight for the Palace. There was a general panic. Everyone screamed and yammered and said it was an omen of defeat. Then someone else rushed in yelling that one griffin had actually reached the Palace and was sliding down the marble front. There was more outcry. The next thing, everyone said, the great gold Angel from the Cathedral would fly away too.

Tonino was taking advantage of the confusion to bash a piece off his roll with the Duke's lighter, when the Duke bellowed, "*Nonsense!*" There was sudden quiet. Tonino dared not move, because everyone was certainly looking at the Duke.

"Don't you see?" said the Duke. "It's just an enemy trick. But we in Caprona don't frighten that easily, do we? Here – you – go and fetch the Montanas. And you go and get the Petrocchis. Tell them it's urgent. Tell as many of them to come as possible. I shall be in the North gallery." And he went striding off there, while Angelica and Tonino jigged against bread and tried not to tread in the butter.

When he got to the gallery, the Duke sat down on a window-seat. Angelica and Tonino stood half out of his pockets and managed to eat their bread and butter. The Duke amiably handed the cigar-cutter from one to the other and, in between whiles, seemed lost in thought, staring at the white puffs of shells bursting on the hills behind Caprona.

Angelica was inclined to be smug. "I told you," she said to Tonino, "my spells always work."

"Iron griffins," said Tonino, "aren't mice."

"No, but I've never done anything as big as that before," said Angelica. "I'm glad it didn't knock the Palace down."

The Duke said gloomily, "The guns of Pisa are going to do that soon. I can see gunboats on the river, and I'm sure they aren't ours. I wish your families would be quick."

But it was half an hour before a polite footman came up to the Duke, causing him to flip his pocket-flaps down and scatter buttery crumbs in all directions.

"Your Grace, members of the Montana and Petrocchi

families are awaiting you in the Large Reception Saloon."

"Good!" said the Duke. He leapt up and ran so fast that Tonino and Angelica had to brace their feet on the seams of his pockets and hang on hard to the edges. They lost their footing several times, even though the Duke tried to help them by holding his pockets as he ran. They felt him clatter to a stop. "Blast!" he said. "This is always happening!"

"What?" asked Tonino breathlessly. He felt jerked out of shape.

"They've told me the wrong room!" said the Duke and set off again on another swaying, jolting run. They felt him dive forward through a doorway. His pockets swung. Then they swung the other way as he slid and stopped. "Lucrezia, this is too bad! Is this why you always tell me the wrong room?"

"My lord," came the coldest voice of the Duchess from some way off, "I can't answer for the slackness of the footmen. What is the matter?"

"This," said the Duke. "These—" They felt him shaking. "Those were the Montanas and the Petrocchis, weren't they? Don't fob me off, Lucrezia. I sent for them. I know."

"And what if they were?" said the Duchess, rather nearer. "Do you wish to join them, my lord?"

They felt the Duke backing away. "No. No indeed! My dear, your will is always my pleasure. I – I just want to know why. They only came about some griffins."

The Duchess's voice moved away again as she answered. "Because, if you must know, Antonio Montana recognised me."

"But – but—" said the Duke, laughing uneasily, "everyone knows you, my dear. You're the Duchess of Caprona."

"I mean, he recognised me for what I am," said the Duchess from the distance. The sound of a door shutting followed.

"Look!" said the Duke in a shaky whisper. "Just look!" While he was still saying it, Angelica and Tonino were bracing their feet on the seams of his pockets and pushing their heads out from under the flaps.

They saw the same polished room where they had once waited and eaten cakes, the same gilded chairs and angelic ceiling. But this time the polished floor was littered with puppets. Puppets lay all over it, limp grotesque things, scattered this way and that as people might lie if they had suddenly fallen. They were in two groups. Otherwise there was no way of telling which puppet was who. There were Punches, Judys, Hangmen, Sausage-men, Policemen, and an odd Devil or so, over and over again. From the numbers, it looked as if both families had realised that Tonino and Angelica were behind the mysterious griffins and had sent nearly every grown-up in the Casas.

Tonino could not speak. Angelica said, "That hateful woman! Her mind seems to run on puppets."

"She sees people that way," the Duke said miserably. "I'm sorry, both of you. She's been too many for us. Terrible female! I can't think why I married her – but I suppose that was a spell too."

"Do you think she suspects you've got us?" Tonino asked. "She must be wondering where we are."

"Maybe, maybe," said the Duke. He marched up and down the room, while they leant out of his pockets and looked down at the crowd of strewn floppy puppets. "She doesn't care now, of course," he said. "She's done for both families anyway. Oh, I am a fool!"

"It's not your fault," said Angelica.

"Oh, but it *is*," said the Duke. "I never show the slightest resolution. I always take the easiest way— What is it?" Darkness descended as he flipped his pocket-flaps down.

"Your Grace," said the Major whose boots squeaked, "the Pisan fleet is landing men down beyond the New Quays. And our troops to the south are being rolled back into the suburbs."

They felt the Duke droop. "Almost done, in fact," he said. "Thanks— No, wait. Major! Could you be a good fellow and go to the stables and order out my coach? The lackeys have all run away, you know. Ask for it at the door in five minutes."

"But, Your Grace—" said the Major.

"I intend to go down into the city and speak with the people," said the Duke. "Give them what's-it-called. Moral support."

"A very fine aim, sir," said the Major, with a great deal more warmth. "In five minutes, sir." His boots went squeaking swiftly off.

"Did you hear that?" said the Duke. "He called me 'sir'! Poor fellow. I told him a set of whoppers and he couldn't take his eyes off all those puppets, but he called me 'sir', and he'll get that coach and he won't tell *her*. Cardboard box!"

226

The hangings whipped by as the Duke charged through a doorway into another room. This one had a long table down the middle. "Ah!" said the Duke, and charged towards a stack of boxes by the wall. The boxes proved to have wine-glasses in them, which the Duke proceeded feverishly to unload on to the table.

"I don't understand," Tonino said.

"Box," said the Duke. "We can't leave your families behind, for her to revenge herself on. I'm going to be resolute for once. I'm going to get in the coach and go, and dare her to stop me." So saying, he stormed back to the reception room with the empty box and knelt down to collect the puppets. Angelica was bounced on the floor as his coat swung. "Sorry," said the Duke.

"Pick them up gently," said Tonino. "It hurts if you don't."

Tenderly and hastily, using both hands for each puppet, the Duke packed the puppets in layers in the cardboard box. In the process, Montanas got very thoroughly mixed with Petrocchis, but there was no way of preventing that. All three of them were expecting the Duchess to come in any moment. The Duke kept looking nervously round and then muttering to himself "Resolute!" He was still muttering it when he set off awkwardly carrying the cardboard box in his arms. "Funny to think," he remarked, "that I'm carrying almost every spell-maker in Caprona at the moment."

Boots squeaked towards them. "Your coach is waiting, sir," said the voice of the Major.

"Resolute," said the Duke. "I mean, thank you. I shall

think of you in heaven, Major, since I'm sure that's where most of us are going soon. Meanwhile, can you do two more things for me?"

"Sir?" said the Major alertly.

"First, when you think of the Angel of Caprona, what do you think of?"

"The song or the figure, sir?" the Major asked, more wary now than alert.

"The figure."

"Why—" The Major was becoming sure that the Duke was mad again. "I – I think of the golden Angel on the Cathedral, Your Grace."

"Good man!" the Duke cried out. "So do I! The other thing is, can you take this box and stow it in my coach for me?" Neither Tonino nor Angelica could resist peeping out to see how the Major took this request. Unfortunately, his face was hidden behind the box as the Duke thrust it at him. They felt they had missed a rare sight. "If anyone asks," the Duke said, "it's gifts for the war-weary people."

"Yes, Your Grace." The Major sounded amused and indulgent, humouring the Duke in his madness, but they heard his boots squeaking briskly off.

"Thank the lord!" said the Duke. "I'm not going to be caught with them. I can feel her coming."

Thanks to the Duke's charging run, it was some minutes before the Duchess caught up with them. Tonino, squinting out under the flap, could see the great marble entrance hall when the Duke skidded to a stop. He dropped the flap hastily when he heard the cold voice of the Duchess. She sounded out of breath but triumphant.

"The enemy is by the New Bridge, my lord. You'll be killed if you go out now."

"And I'll be killed if I stay here too," said the Duke. He waited for the Duchess to deny this, but she said nothing. They heard the Duke swallow. But his resolution held. "I'm going," he said, a mite squeakily, "to drive down among my people and comfort their remaining hours."

"Sentimental fool," said the Duchess. She was not angry. It was what she thought the Duke was.

This made the Duke bluster. "I may not be a good ruler," he said, "but this is what a good ruler should do. I shall – I shall pat the heads of children and join in the singing of the choir."

The Duchess laughed. "And much good may it do you, particularly if you sing," she said. "Very well. You can get killed down there instead of up here. Run along and pat heads."

"Thank you, my dear," the Duke said humbly. He surged forward again, *thump, thump, thump*, down marble steps. They heard the sound of hooves on gravel and felt the Duke shaking. "Let's go, Carlo," he said. "What is it? What are you pointing—? Oh yes. So it is a griffin. How remarkable. Drive on, can't you?" He surged upwards. Coach springs creaked and a door clapped shut. The Duke surged down. They heard him say "Oh good!" as he sat, and the rather-too-familiar sound of cardboard being hit, as he patted the box on the seat beside him. Then the coach started, with a shrilling of wheels on gravel and a battering of hooves. They felt the Duke sigh with relief. It made them bounce. "You can come out now," said the Duke.

They climbed cautiously out on to his wide knees. The Duke kindly moved over to the window so that they could see out. And the first thing that met their eyes was an iron griffin, very crumpled and bent, lying in quite a large crater in the Palace yard.

"You know," said the Duke, "if my Palace wasn't going to be broken up anyway by Pisans, or Sienese, or Florentines, I'd get damages off you two. The other griffin has scraped two great ditches all down my facade." He laughed and patted at his glossy face with his handkerchief. He was still very nervous.

As the coach rolled out of the yard on to the road, they heard gunfire. Some of it sounded near, a rattle of shots from below by the river. Most of it was far and huge, a long grumble from the hills. The bangs were so close together that the sound was nearly continuous, but every so often, out of the grumble, came a very much nearer *clap-clap-clap*. It made all three of them jump each time.

"We *are* taking a pounding," the Duke said unhappily.

The coach slowed down. They could hear the prim voice of the coachman among the other noise. "I fear the New Bridge is under fire, Your Grace. Where exactly are we bound?"

The Duke pushed down the window. The noise doubled. "The Cathedral. Go upriver and see if we can cross by the Old Bridge." He pushed the window shut. "Phew! I don't envy Carlo up there on the box!"

"Why are we going to the Cathedral?" Angelica asked anxiously. "We want to look at the Angels on our Casas."

"No," said the Duke. "She'll have thought of those.

That's why I asked the Major. It seems to me that the one place where those words are always safe and always invisible *must* be on the Cathedral Angel. You think of it at once, but it's up there and far away, so you forget it."

"But it's *miles* up!" said Angelica.

"It's got a scroll, though," said Tonino. "And the scroll looks to be more unrolled than the ones on our Angels."

"I'm afraid it's bound to be about the only place she might have forgotten," said the Duke.

They rattled along briskly, except for one place, where there was a shell crater in the road. Somehow, Carlo got them round it.

"Good man, Carlo," said the Duke. "About the one good man she hasn't got rid of."

The noise diminished a little as the coach went down to the river and the Piazza Martia – at least, Angelica and Tonino guessed that was where it was; they found they were too small to see any great distance. They could tell they were on the Old Bridge, by the rumble under the wheels and the little shuttered houses on either side. The Duke several times craned round, whistled and shook his head, but they could not see why. They recognised the Cathedral, when the coach wheeled towards it across the cobbles, because it was so huge and snowy white. Its great bell was still tolling. A large crowd, mostly of women and children, was slowly moving towards its door. As the coach drew up, it was near enough for Tonino and Angelica to see the Archbishop of Caprona in his spreading robes, standing at the door, sprinkling each person with holy water and murmuring a blessing.

"Now there's a brave man," said the Duke. "I wish I could do as well. Look, I'll pop you two out of this door and then get out of the other one and keep everyone busy while you get up on the dome. Will that do?" He had the door nearest the Cathedral open as he spoke.

Tonino and Angelica felt lost and helpless. "But what shall we do?"

"Climb up there and read out those words," said the Duke. He leant down, encircled them with his warm wet hands, and planted them out on the cold cobbles. They stood shivering under the vast hoop of the coach-wheel. "Be sensible," he whispered down to them. "If I ask the Archbishop to put up ladders, she'll guess." That of course was quite true. They heard him surge to the other door and that door crash open.

"He always does everything so *hugely*," Angelica said.

"People of Caprona!" shouted the Duke. "I've come here to be with you in your hour of sorrow. Believe me, I didn't choose what has happened today—"

There was a mutter from the crowd, even a scatter of cheering. "He's doing it quite well," said Angelica.

"We'd better do our bit," said Tonino. "There's only us left now."

CHAPTER FIFTEEN

✳

*T*onino and Angelica pattered over to the vast marble cliff of the Cathedral and doubtfully approached a long, sloping buttress. That was the only thing they could see which gave them some chance of climbing up. Once they were close to it, they saw it was not difficult at all. The marble looked smooth, but, to people as small as they were, it was rough enough to give a grip to their hands and feet.

They went up like monkeys, with the cold air reviving them. The truth was that, though they had had an eventful morning, it had also been a restful and stuffy one. They were full of energy and they weighed no more than a few ounces. They were scarcely panting as they scampered up the long cold slope of the lowest dome. But there the rest of the Cathedral rose before them, a complicated glacier of white and rose and green marble. They could not see the Angel at all.

Neither of them knew which way to climb next. They hung on to a golden cross and stared up. And there, brown-black hair and white fur hurtled up to them. Gold eyes glared and blue eyes gazed. A black nose and a pink nose dabbed at them.

"Benvenuto!" shouted Tonino. "Did you—?"

"Vittoria!" cried Angelica, and threw her arms round the neck of the white cat.

But the cats were hasty and very worried. Things tumbled into their heads, muddled, troubled things about Paolo and Renata, Marco and Rosa. Would Tonino and Angelica please come on, and *hurry*!

They began an upward scamper which they would never have believed possible. With the cats to guide them, they raced up long lead groins, and over rainbow buttresses, like dizzy bridges, to higher domes. Always the cats implored them to hurry, and always they were there if the footing was difficult. With his hand on Benvenuto's wiry back, Tonino went gaily up marble glacis and through tiny drain-holes hanging over huge drops, and raced up high curving surfaces, where the green marble ribs of a dome seemed as tall as a wall beside him. Even when they began the long toil up the slope of the great dome itself, neither of them was troubled. Once, Angelica stumbled and saved herself by catching hold of Vittoria's silky tail; and once Benvenuto took Tonino's red nightgown in his teeth and heaved him aside from a deep drain. But up here it was rounded and remote. Tonino felt as if he was on the surface of the moon, in spite of the pale winter sky overhead and the wind singing. The rumble of guns was almost beyond the scope of his small ears.

At last, they scrambled between fat marble pillars on to the platform at the very top of the dome. And there was the golden Angel above them. The Angel's tremendous feet rested on a golden pedestal rather higher than Tonino's normal height. There was a design round the pedestal, which Tonino absently took in, of golden leopards entwined with winged horses. But he was looking up beyond, to the Angel's flowing robes, the enormous wings outspread to a width of twenty feet or more, the huge hand high above his head, raised in blessing, and the other hand flung out against the sky, further away still, holding the great unrolled scroll. Far above that again, shone the Angel's vast and tranquil face, unheedingly beaming its blessing over Caprona.

"He's enormous!" Angelica said. "We'll never get up to that scroll, if we try all day!"

The cats, however, were nudging and hustling at them, to come to a place further round the platform. Wondering, they trotted round, almost under the Angel's scroll. And there was Paolo's head above the balustrade, with his hair blown back in a tuft and his face exceedingly pale. He had one arm clutched over the marble railing. The other stretched away downward. Tonino peered between the marble pillars to see why. And there was the miserable humped huddle of Renata hanging on to Paolo.

"But she's terrified of heights!" said Angelica. "How *did* she get this high?"

Vittoria told Angelica she was to get Renata up at once.

Angelica stuck her upper half out between the pillars. Being small certainly had its advantages. Distances which were mercilessly huge to Renata and Paolo were too far away to worry Angelica. The dome was like a whole small world to her.

Paolo said, carefully patient, "I can't hold on much longer. Do you think you can have another try?" The answer from Renata was a sobbing shudder.

"Renata!" shouted Angelica.

Renata's scared face turned slowly up. "Something's happened to my eyes now! You look tiny."

"I *am* tiny!" yelled Angelica.

"Both of them are!" Paolo said, staring at Tonino's head.

"Pull me up quick," said Renata. The size of Angelica and Tonino so worried Renata and Paolo that both of them forgot they were hundreds of feet in the air. Paolo heaved on Renata and Renata shoved at Paolo, and they scrambled over the marble rail in a second. But there, Renata looked up at the immense golden Angel and had an instant relapse. "Oh – oh!" she wailed and sank down in a heap against the golden pedestal.

Tonino and Angelica huddled behind her. The warmth of climbing had worn off. They were feeling the wind keenly through their scanty nightshirts.

Benvenuto leapt across Renata to them. Something else had to be done, and done quickly.

Tonino went again and looked through the marble pillars, where the dome curved away and down like an ice-field with ribs of green and gold. There, coming into view over the curve, was a bright red uniform, making Marco's carroty hair look faded and sallow against it. The uniform went with Marco's hair even less well than the crimson he had worn as a coachman. Tonino knew who Marco was in that instant. But that bothered him less than seeing Marco flattened to the surface and looking backwards, which Tonino was sure was a mistake. Beyond Marco's boots, fair hair was wildly blowing. Rosa's flushed face came into sight.

"I'm all *right*. Look after yourself," Rosa said.

Benvenuto was beside Tonino. They were to come up quicker than that. It was important.

"Get Rosa and Marco up here quickly!" Tonino shrieked to Paolo. He did not know if he had caught the feeling from the cats or not, but he was sure Rosa and Marco were in danger.

Paolo went unwillingly to the railing and flinched at the height. "They've been following us and shouting the whole way," he said. "Get up here quickly!" he shouted.

"Thank you very much!" Marco shouted back. "Whose fault is it we're up here anyway?"

"Is Renata all right?" Rosa yelled.

Angelica and Tonino pushed themselves between the pillars. "Hurry up!" they screamed.

The sight of them worked on Rosa and Marco as it had done on Renata and Paolo. They stared at the two tiny figures, and got to their feet as they stared. Then, stooping over, with their hands hanging, they came racing up the last of the curve for a closer look. Marco tumbled over the rail and said, as he was pulling Rosa over, "I couldn't believe my eyes at first! We'd better do a growing-spell before—"

"Get down!" said Paolo. Benvenuto's message was so urgent that he had caught it too. Both cats were crouching, still and low, and even Benvenuto's flat ears were flattened. Rosa stooped down. Marco grudgingly went on one knee.

"Look here, Paolo—" he began.

A savage gale hit the dome. Freezing wind shrieked across the platform, howled in the spaces between the marble pillars, and scoured across the curve of the dome below. The Angel's wings thrummed with it. It brought stabs of rain and needles of ice, hurling so hard that Tonino was thrown flat on his face. He could hear ice rattling on the Angel and spitting on the dome. Paolo snatched him into shelter behind himself. Renata feebly scrabbled about until she found Angelica and dragged her into shelter by one arm. Marco and Rosa bowed over. It was quite clear that anyone climbing the dome would have been blown off.

The wind passed, wailing like a wolf. They raised their heads into the sun.

The Duchess was standing on the platform in front of them. She had melting ice winking and trickling from her hair and from every fold of her marble-grey dress. The smile on her waxy face was not pleasant.

"Oh no," she said. "The Angel is not going to help anyone this time. Did you think I'd forgotten?"

Marco and Rosa looked up at the Angel's golden arm

holding the great scroll above them. If they had not understood before, they knew now. From their suddenly thoughtful faces, Tonino knew they were finding spells to use on the Duchess.

"Don't!" squeaked Angelica. "She's an enchantress!"

The Duchess's lips pursed in another unpleasant little smile. "More than that," she said. She pointed up at the Angel. "Let the words be removed from the scroll," she said.

There was a click from the huge golden statue, followed by a grating sound, as if a spring had been released. The arm holding the scroll began to move, gently and steadily downwards, making the slightest grinding noise as it moved. They could hear it easily, in spite of a sudden clatter of gunfire from the houses beyond the river. Downwards and inwards, travelled the Angel's arm, until it stopped with a small *clunk*. The scroll now hung, flashing in the sun, between them and the Duchess. There were large raised letters on it. *Angelus*, they saw. *Capronensi populo*. It was as if the Angel were holding it out for them to read.

"Exactly," said the Duchess, though Tonino thought, from the surprised arch of her eyebrows, that this was not at all what she expected. She pointed again at the scroll, with a long white finger like a white wax pencil. "Erase," she said. "Word by word."

Their heads all tipped anxiously as they looked at the lines of writing. The first word read *Carmen*. And, sure enough, the golden capital C was sinking slowly away into the metal background. Paolo moved. He had to do something. The Duchess glanced at him, a contemptuous flick of the eyebrows. Paolo found he was twisted to the spot, with jabbing cramp in both legs.

But he could still speak, and he remembered what Marco and Rosa had said last night. Without daring to draw breath, he screamed as loud as he could. "*Chrestomanci!*"

There was more wind. This was one keen blaring gust. And Chrestomanci was there, beyond Renata and the cats. There was so little room on the platform that Chrestomanci rocked, and quickly took hold of the marble balustrade. He was still in uniform, but it was muddy and he looked extremely tired.

The Duchess whirled round and pointed her long finger at him. "You! I misled you!"

"Oh you did," Chrestomanci said. If the Duchess had hoped to catch him off balance, she was too late. Chrestomanci was steady now. "You led me a proper wild-goose-chase," he said, and put out one hand, palm forwards, towards her pointing finger. The long finger bent and began dripping white, as if it were wax indeed. The Duchess stared at it, and then looked up at Chrestomanci almost imploringly. "No," Chrestomanci said, sounding very tired. "I think you've done enough harm. Take your true form, please." He beckoned at her, like someone sick of waiting.

Instantly, the Duchess's body was seething out of shape. Her arms gathered inwards. Her face lengthened, and yet still remained the same waxy, sardonic face. Whiskers sprang from her upper lip, and her eyes lit red, like bulging lamps. Her marble skirts turned white, billowed and gathered soapily to her ankles, revealing her feet as long pink claws. And all the time, she was shrinking. Two teeth appeared at the end of her lengthened white face. A naked pink tail, marked in rings like an earthworm, snaked from behind the soapy bundle of her skirts and lashed the marble floor angrily. She shrank again.

Finally a huge white rat with eyes like red marbles, leapt to the marble railing and crouched, chittering and glaring with its humped back twitching.

"The White Devil," said Chrestomanci, "which the Angel was sent to expel from Caprona. Right, Benvenuto and Vittoria. She's all yours. Make sure she never comes back."

Benvenuto and Vittoria were already creeping forward. Their tails swept about and their eyes stared. They sprang. The rat sprang too, off the parapet with a squeal, and went racing away down the dome. Benvenuto raced with it, long and low, keeping just beside the pink whip of its tail. Vittoria raced the other side, a snowy sliver making the great rat look yellow, running at the rat's shoulder. They saw the rat turn and try to bite her. And then, suddenly, the three were joined by a dozen smaller rats, all running and squealing. They only saw them for an instant, before the whole group ran over the slope of the dome and disappeared.

"Her helpers from the Palace," said Chrestomanci.

"Will Vittoria be safe?" said Angelica.

"She's the best ratter in Caprona, isn't she?" said Chrestomanci. "Apart from Benvenuto, that is. And by the time the Devil and her friends get to the ground, they'll have every cat in Caprona after them. Now—"

Tonino found he was the right size again. He clung to Rosa's hand. Beyond Rosa, he could see Angelica, also the right size, shivering and pulling her flimsy blue dress down over her knees, before she grabbed for Marco's hand. The wind was far worse on a larger body. But what made Tonino grab at Rosa was not that. The dome was not world-sized any more. It was a white hummock wheeling in a grey-brown landscape. The hills round Caprona were pitilessly clear. He could see flashes of flame and running figures which seemed to be almost beside him, or just above him, as if the tiny white dome had reeled over on its side. Yet the houses of Caprona were immeasurably deep below, and the river seemed to stand up out of them. The New Bridge appeared almost overhead, suffused in clouds of smoke. Smoke rolled in the hills and swirled giddily out of the downside-upside houses beyond the Old Bridge, and, worst of all, the boom and clap, the rattle and yammer of guns was now nearly deafening. Tonino no longer wondered what had scared Renata and Paolo so. He felt as if he was spinning to his death.

He clung to Rosa's hand and looked desperately up at the Angel. That at least was still huge. The scroll, which it still held patiently towards them, was almost as big as the side of a house.

"—Now," said Chrestomanci, "the best thing you can do, all of you, is to sing those words, quickly."

"What? Me too?" said Angelica.

"Yes, all of you," said Chrestomanci.

They gathered, the six of them, against the marble parapet, facing the golden scroll, with the New Bridge behind them, and began, somewhat uncertainly, to fit those words to the tune of the *Angel of Caprona*. They matched like a glove. As soon as they realised this, everyone sang lustily. Angelica and Renata stopped shivering. Tonino let go of Rosa's hand, and Rosa put her arm over his shoulders instead. And they sang as if they had always known those words. It was only a version of the usual words in Latin, but it was what the tune had always asked for.

> *"Carmen pacis saeculare*
> *Venit Angelus cantare,*
> *Et deorsum pacem dare*
> > *Capronensi populo.*
>
> *Dabit pacem eternalem,*
> *Sine morbo immortalem,*
> *Sine pugna triumphalem,*
> > *Capronensi populo.*
>
> *En diabola albata*
> *De Caprona expulsata,*
> *Missa pax et virtus data*
> > *Capronensi populo."*

When they had finished, there was silence. There was not a sound from the hills, or the New Bridge, or the streets below. Every noise had stopped. So they were all the more startled at the tinny slithering with which the Angel slowly rolled up the scroll. The shining outstretched wings bent and settled against the Angel's golden shoulders, where the Angel gave them a shake to order the feathers. And that noise was not the sound of metal, but the softer rattling of real pinions. It brought with it a scent of such sweetness that there was a moment when they were not aware of anything else.

In that moment, the Angel was in flight. As the huge golden wings passed over them, the scent came again and, with it, the sound of singing. It seemed like hundreds of voices, singing tune, harmony and descant to the *Angel of Caprona*. They had no idea if it was the Angel alone, or something else. They looked up and watched the golden figure wheel and soar and wheel, until it was only a golden glint in the sky. And there was still utter silence, except for the singing.

Rosa sighed. "I suppose we'd better climb down." Renata began to shiver again at the thought.

Chrestomanci sighed too. "Don't worry about that."

They were suddenly down again, on solid cobbles, in the Cathedral forecourt. The Cathedral was once more a great white building, the houses were high, the hills were away beyond, and the people surrounding them were anything but quiet. Everyone was running to where they could see the Angel, flashing in the sun as he soared. The Archbishop was in tears, and so was the Duke. They were wringing one another's hands beside the Duke's coach.

And Chrestomanci had brought them to earth in time to see another miracle. The coach began to work and bounce on its springs. Both doors burst open. Aunt Francesca squeezed out of one, and Guido Petrocchi fell out after her. From the other door tumbled Rinaldo and the red-haired Petrocchi aunt. After them came mingled Montanas and Petrocchis, more and more and more, until anyone could see that the coach could not possibly have held that number. People stopped crowding to see the Angel and crowded to look at the Duke's coach instead.

Rosa and Marco looked at one another and began to back away among the spectators. But Chrestomanci took them each by a shoulder. "It'll be all right," he said. "And if it isn't, I'll set you up in a spell-house in Venice."

Antonio disentangled himself from a Petrocchi uncle and hurried with Guido towards Tonino and Angelica. "Are you all right?" both of them said. "Was it you who fetched the griffins—?" They broke off to stare coldly at one another.

"Yes," said Tonino. "I'm sorry you were turned into puppets."

"She was too clever for us," said Angelica. "But be thankful you got your proper clothes back afterwards. Look at us. We—"

They were pulled apart then by aunts and cousins, fearing they were contaminating one another, and hurriedly given coats and sweaters by uncles. Paolo was swept away from Renata too, by Aunt Maria. "Don't go near her, my love!"

"Oh well," said Renata, as she was pulled away too. "Thanks for helping me up the dome, anyway."

"Just a moment!" Chrestomanci said loudly. Everyone turned to him, respectful but irritable. "If each spell-house," he said, "insists on regarding the other as monsters, I can promise you that Caprona will shortly fall again." They stared at him, Montanas and Petrocchis, equally indignant. The Archbishop looked at the Duke, and both of them began to edge towards the shelter of the Cathedral porch.

"What are you talking about?" Rinaldo said aggressively. His dignity was damaged by being a puppet anyway. The look in his eye seemed to promise cowpats for everyone – with the largest share for Chrestomanci.

"I'm talking about the Angel of Caprona," said Chrestomanci. "When the Angel alighted on the Cathedral, in the time of the First Duke of Caprona, bearing the safety of Caprona with him, history clearly states that the Duke appointed two men – Antonio Petrocchi and Piero Montana – to be keepers of the words of the Angel and therefore keepers of the safety of Caprona. In memory of this, each Casa has an Angel over its gate, and the great Angel stands on a pedestal showing the Petrocchi leopard entwined with the Montana winged horse." Chrestomanci pointed upwards. "If you don't believe me, ask for ladders and go and see. Antonio Petrocchi and Piero Montana were fast friends, and so were their families after them. There were frequent marriages between the two Casas. And Caprona became a great city and a strong State. Its decline dates from that ridiculous quarrel between Ricardo and Francesco."

There were murmurs from Montanas and Petrocchis alike, here, that the quarrel was *not* ridiculous.

"Of course it was," said Chrestomanci. "You've all been deceived from your cradles up. You've let Ricardo and Francesco fool you for two centuries. What they really quarrelled about we shall never know, but I know they both told their families the same lies. And you have all gone on believing their lies and getting deeper and deeper divided, until the White Devil was actually able to enter Caprona again."

Again there were murmurs. Antonio said, "The Duchess *was* the White Devil, but—"

"Yes," said Chrestomanci. "And she has gone for the moment, because the words were found and the Angel awakened by members of both families. I suspect it could only have been done by Montanas and Petrocchis united. The rest of you could have sung the right words separately, until you were all blue in the face, and nothing would have happened. The Angel respects only friendship. The young ones of both families are luckily less bigoted than the rest of you. Marco and Rosa have even had the courage to fall in love and get married—"

Up till then, both families had listened – restively, it was true, because it was not pleasant to be lectured in front of a crowd of fellow citizens, not to speak of the Duke and the Archbishop – but they had listened. But at this, pandemonium broke out.

"*Married!*" screamed the Montanas. "She's a *Montana!*" screamed the Petrocchis. Insults were yelled at Rosa and at Marco. Anyone who wished to count would have found no less than ten aunts in tears at once, and all cursing as they wept.

Rosa and Marco were both white. It needed only Rinaldo to step up to Marco, glowering, and he did. "This scum," he said to Rosa, "knocked me down and cut my head open. And you marry it!"

Chrestomanci made haste to get between Marco and Rinaldo. "I'd hoped someone would see reason," he said to Rosa. He seemed very tired. "It had better be Venice."

"Get out of my way!" said Rinaldo. "You double-dealing sorcerer!"

"Please move, sir," said Marco. "I don't need to be shielded from an idiot like him."

"Marco," said Chrestomanci, "have you thought what two families of powerful magicians could do to you and Rosa?"

"Of course we have!" Marco said angrily, trying to push Chrestomanci aside.

But a strange silence fell again, the silence of the Angel. The Archbishop knelt down. Awed people crowded to one side or another of the Cathedral yard. The Angel was returning. He came from far off down the Corso, on foot now, with his wing-tips brushing the cobbles and the chorus of voices swelling as he approached. As he passed through the Cathedral court, it was seen that in every place where a feather had touched the stones there grew a cluster of small golden flowers. Scent gushed over everyone as the Angel drew near and halted by the Cathedral porch, towering and golden.

There he turned his remote smiling face to everyone present. His voice was like one voice singing above many. "Caprona is at peace. Keep our covenant."

At that he spread his wings, making them all dizzy with the scent. And he was next seen moving upwards, over lesser domes and greater, to take his place once more on the great dome, guarding Caprona in the years to come.

This is really the end of the story, except for one or two explanations.

Marco and Rosa had to tell their story many times, at least as often as Tonino and Angelica told theirs. Among the first people they told it to was Old Niccolo, who was lying restlessly in bed and only kept there because Elizabeth sat beside him all the time. "But I'm quite well!" he kept saying.

So, in order to keep him there, Elizabeth had first Tonino and then Rosa and Marco come and tell him their stories.

Rosa and Marco had met when they were both working on the Old Bridge. Falling in love and deciding to marry had been the easiest part, over in minutes. The difficulty was that they had to provide themselves with a family each which had nothing to do with either Casa. Rosa contrived a family first. She pretended to be English. She became very friendly with the English girl at the Art Gallery – the same Jane Smith that Rinaldo fancied so much. Jane Smith thought it was a great joke to pretend to be Rosa's sister. She wrote long letters in English to Guido Petrocchi, supposed to be from Rosa's English father, and visited the Casa Petrocchi herself the day Rosa was introduced there.

Rosa and Marco planned the introductions carefully. They used the pear-tree spell – which they worked together

– in both Casas, to Jane's amusement. But the Petrocchis, though they liked the pear-tree, were not kind to Rosa at first. In fact, some of Marco's aunts were so unpleasant that Marco was quite disgusted with them. That was why Marco was able to tell Antonio so vehemently that he hated the Petrocchis. But the aunts became used to Rosa in time. Renata and Angelica became very fond of her. And the wedding was held just after Christmas.

All this time, Marco had been unable to find anyone to act as a family for him. He was in despair. Then, only a few days before the wedding, his father sent him with a message to the house of Mario Andretti, the builder. And Marco discovered that the Andrettis had a blind daughter. When Marco asked, Mario Andretti said he would do anything for anyone who cured his daughter.

"Even then, we hardly dared hope," said Marco. "We didn't know if we could cure her."

"And apart from that," said Rosa, "the only time we dared both go there was the night after the wedding."

So the wedding was held in the Casa Petrocchi. Jane Smith helped Rosa make her dress and was a bridesmaid for her, together with Renata, Angelica and one of Marco's cousins.

Jane thoroughly enjoyed the wedding and seemed, Rosa said dryly, to find Marco's cousin Alberto at least as attractive as Rinaldo, whereas Rosa and Marco could think of almost nothing but little Maria Andretti. They hurried to the Andrettis' house as soon as the celebrations were over.

"And I've never known anything so difficult," said Rosa. "We were at it all night!"

Elizabeth was unable to contain herself here. "And I never even knew you were out!" she said.

"We took good care you didn't," said Rosa. "Anyway, we hadn't done anything like that before, so we had to look up spells in the University. We tried seventeen and none of them worked. In the end we had to make up one of our own. And all the time, I was thinking: suppose this doesn't work on the poor child either, and we've played with the Andrettis' hopes."

"Not to speak of our own," said Marco. "Then our spell worked. Maria yelled out that the room was all colours and there were things like trees in it – she thought people looked like trees – and we all jumped about in the dawn, hugging one another. And Andretti was as good as his word, and did his brother-act so well here that I told him he ought to be on the stage."

"He took *me* in," Old Niccolo said, wonderingly.

"But someone was bound to find out in the end," said Elizabeth. "What did you mean to do then?"

"Just hoped," said Marco. "We thought perhaps people might get used to it—"

"In other words, you behaved like a couple of young idiots," said Old Niccolo. "What is that terrible stench?" And he leapt up and raced out on to the gallery to investigate, with Elizabeth, Rosa and Marco racing after him to stop him.

The smell, of course, was the kitchen-spell again. The insects had vanished and a smell of drains had taken their place. All day long, the kitchen belched out stinks, which grew stronger towards evening. It was particularly unfortunate, because the whole of Caprona was preparing to feast and celebrate. Caprona was truly at peace. The troops from Florence, and Pisa and Siena, had all returned home – somewhat bewildered and wondering how they had been beaten – and the people of Caprona were dancing in the streets.

"And we can't even cook, let alone celebrate!" wailed Aunt Gina.

Then an invitation arrived from the Casa Petrocchi. Would the Casa Montana be pleased to join in the celebrations at the Casa Petrocchi? It was a trifle stiff, but the Casa Montana did please. What could be more fortunate? Tonino and Paolo suspected that it was Chrestomanci's doing.

The only difficulty was to stop Old Niccolo getting out of bed and going with the rest of them. Everyone said Elizabeth had done enough. Everyone, even Aunt Francesca, wanted to go.

Then, more fortunately still, Uncle Umberto turned up, and old Luigi Petrocchi with him. They said they would sit with Old Niccolo – and on him if necessary. They were too old for dancing.

So everyone else went to the Casa Petrocchi, and it proved a celebration to remember. The Duke was there, because Angelica had insisted on it. The Duke was so grateful to be invited that he had brought with him as much wine and as many cakes as his coach would hold, and six footmen in a second coach to serve it.

"The Palace is awful," he said. "No one in it but Punch and Judys. Somehow I don't fancy them like I used to."

What with the wine, the cakes, and the good food baked in the Casa Petrocchi kitchen, the evening became very merry. Somebody found a barrel-organ and everyone danced to it in the yard. And, if the six footmen forgot to serve cakes and danced with the rest, who was to blame them? After all, the Duke was dancing with Aunt Francesca – a truly formidable sight.

Tonino sat with Paolo and Renata beside a charcoal brazier, watching the dancing. And while they sat, Benvenuto suddenly emerged from the shadows and sat down by the brazier, where he proceeded to give himself a fierce and thorough wash.

They had done a fine, enjoyable job on that white rat, he informed Tonino, as he stuck one leg high above his gnarled head and subjected it to punishing tongue-work. She'd not be back again.

"But is Vittoria all right?" Renata wanted to know.

Fine, was Benvenuto's answer. She was resting. She was going to have kittens. They would be particularly good kittens because Benvenuto was the father. Tonino was to make sure to get one for the Casa Montana.

Tonino asked Renata for a kitten then and there, and Renata promised to ask Angelica. Whereupon, Benvenuto, having worked over both hind legs, wafted himself on to Tonino's knees, where he made himself into a tight brown mat and slept for an hour.

"I wish I could understand him," said Paolo. "He tried to tell me where you were, but all I did was see a picture of the front of the Palace."

"But that's how he always tells things!" said Tonino.

He was surprised Paolo had not known. "You just have to read his pictures."

"What's he saying now?" Renata asked Paolo.

"Nothing," said Paolo. "Snore, snore." And they all laughed.

Sometime later, when Benvenuto had woken up and drifted off to try his luck in the kitchen, Tonino wandered in to a room nearby, without quite knowing why he did. As soon as he got inside, though, he knew it was no accident. Chrestomanci was there, with Angelica and Guido Petrocchi, and so was Antonio. Antonio was looking so worried that Tonino braced himself for trouble.

"We were discussing you, Tonino," said Chrestomanci. "You helped Angelica fetch the griffins, didn't you?"

"Yes," said Tonino. He remembered the damage they had done and felt alarmed.

"And you helped in the kitchen spell?" asked Chrestomanci.

Tonino said "Yes" again. Now he was sure there was trouble.

"And when you hanged the Duchess," Chrestomanci said, to Tonino's confusion, "how did you do that?"

Tonino wondered how he could be in trouble over that too, but he answered, "By doing what the puppet show made me do. I couldn't get out of it, so I had to go along with it, you see."

"I do," said Chrestomanci, and he turned to Antonio rather triumphantly. "You see? And that was the White Devil! What interests me is that it was someone else's spell each time." Then before Tonino could be too puzzled, he turned back to him. "Tonino," he said, "it seems to me that you have a new and rather useful talent. You may not be able to work many spells on your own, but you seem to be able to turn other people's magic to your own use. I think if they had let you help on the Old Bridge, for instance, it would have been mended in half a day. I've been asking your father if he'd let you come back to England with me, so that we could find out just what you can do."

Tonino looked at his father's worried face. He hardly knew what to think. "Not for good?" he said.

Antonio smiled. "Only for a few weeks," he said. "If Chrestomanci's right, we'll need you here badly."

Tonino smiled too. "Then I don't mind," he said.

"But," said Angelica, "it was me who fetched the griffins really."

"What were you really fetching?" asked Guido.

Angelica hung her head. "Mice." She looked resigned when her father roared with laughter.

"I wanted to talk about you too," said Chrestomanci. He said to Guido, "Her spells always work, don't they? It occurs to me you might learn from Angelica."

Guido scratched his beard. "How to turn things green and get griffins, you mean?"

Chrestomanci picked up his glass of wine. "There are risks, of course, to Angelica's methods. But I meant she can show you that a thing need not be done in the same old way in order to work. I think, in time, she will make you a whole new set of spells. Both houses can learn from her." He raised his wine glass.

"Your health, Angelica. Tonino. The Duchess thought

she was getting the weakest members of both Casas, and it turned out quite the opposite."

Antonio and Guido raised their glasses too. "I'll say this," said Guido. "But for you two, we wouldn't be celebrating tonight."

Angelica and Tonino looked at each other and made faces. They felt very shy and very, very pleased.